"LOVERS ARE NOT PEOPLE," SHELLEY THOUGHT...

They are the dreaming spirits within us that awake and take possession of our bodies. I do not know where they come from for at times their beauty is such that I wonder how mere people have created them.

But when that sad time comes, I don't know where they go either. Maybe, like the fools we are, we drive them out, preferring our dull sanity to this manic possession.

David and I were not yet depossessed but we had, imperceptibly, edged toward becoming people once again...

LOVERS ARE NOT PEOPLE

TIMERI MURARI

j

A JOVE BOOK

Copyright © 1977 by Timeri Murari
Published by arrangement with William Morrow and Company, Inc.

All rights reserved. No part of this publication may be reproduced or transmitted in any form or by any means, electronic or mechanical, including photocopy, recording, or any information storage and retrieval system, without permission in writing from the publisher.

Printed in the United States of America

Library of Congress Catalog Card Number: 77-21528

First Jove edition published July 1979

Jove books are published by Jove Publications, Inc., 200 Madison Avenue, New York, N.Y. 10016

FOR MOLLY

SO SPECIAL,

WITH LOVE

WITH MANY THANKS TO . . .

Sabina Iardella

Dick Duane

Bob Thixton

Renni Browne

. . . FOR THEIR ENORMOUS HELP

AND ENCOURAGEMENT

CHAPTER 1

IT WAS ONE O'CLOCK ON A SATURDAY MORNING, FIFTY-one days after he'd left me, that I decided to get my David back.

The boy embracing me, his mouth glued to mine as if administering artificial respiration, interrupted the thought. His foot on my toe didn't help either. I stepped back to avoid suffocation from the sour-sweet odor of his after-shave.

"God, you're beautiful, Shelley."

It didn't sound as romantic as he'd meant it to; he was choking trying to get his tie and jacket off at the same time. If he'd had enough arms he would have been stripped in five seconds. In bed he would be like most young men: all arms, legs, fingers, enthusiasm and premature ejaculations.

"Thank you," moving farther out of reach.

I didn't like the bedroom, so clearly designed for quick seductions. The weak orange glow made us look blurred, and the music was too sweet. The light bowl hung like a street lamp above my head. In our bedroom at home there was a small, delicate chandelier.

His bare arm reached over and across my neck; his

whispering mouth pressed against my ear. I wasn't listening. The hand fell too casually to my breast and rested there, kneading. The other fumbled with my zipper.

"I can do it . . . Gerry."

I hadn't forgotten his name completely; it had just slipped my mind for a moment. I had met him only a few hours ago, at his mother's. I wasn't due for an invitation for another six months, but she had undoubtedly heard of David's desertion and welcomed the opportunity to practice her compassion and, of course, to hear the details.

I wouldn't have gone, but the house and children were like wounds in my side, hurting, and the cocktails and cocktail chatter might prove curative. I had promised myself not to let Marion Keating's pity make me talk, but talk I did. The telling eased some of the familiar, poisonous pressure: the suddenness of David's leaving, the details of his half-read note, the peculiar emotional mixture of bafflement and sudden rages. Gerry Keating had been there and heard and pounced. I couldn't blame him really. I needed him, if only for spite.

Except that David, wherever he was, would see nei-

ther the boy on top of me nor my own humiliation . . . Shelley, drained and numb. And also, alone. I could have a hundred men and it would be the same. I'd feel as if I were in a coffin, a million miles from the nearest human and traveling at the speed of light into darkness.

Oh god, how I missed David. His arms felt different, strong and secure, and when he moved in the night, I felt comforted. His voice could reach inside my frightened heart and put it to rest. Even his sleepy grunt could vibrate me into peace. Some lucky bitch, does she appreciate it? Now hears him grunt while I hear silence?

10

She'd best enjoy him as best she can; she isn't going to have him for long.

I turned, needing to hurry. Gerry was standing naked by the side of the bed, wearing an anticipatory erection. He had a pleasant body with a flat belly, heavily muscled thighs, and the right muscles to give his chest depth and shape. At this moment, it all left me quite dry. He climbed into bed and slid to one side. I picked up my purse and my wrap and went to him.

"You're *leaving*?"

He sat up.

"Yes."

"You must be joking."

It would take too long to explain to the child. I kissed him on the forehead.

"I'm not," stroking his head. "And it's nothing to do with you." He could interpret that any way he liked.

I could feel his hand moving up between my legs, a finger trying to probe through the nylon.

"Don't you dare poke a hole in my tights." That was the last place I wanted a draft.

"Come to bed."

"I have to go home."

"When am I seeing you again?"

"Any time. But not for bed."

I could see him thinking. The start and finish of his easy fuck—a good one too I should add, for I know everything there is to know about fucking. David taught me well.

"How about one for the road?"

My god . . . I was a pint of beer and someone up there had called closing time!

"Jerk off." Not unkindly.

The corridor of the flat was colder than the room. I finally found the door after walking into a closet, the bathroom, and the kitchen. I took the elevator down and skipped past the doorman.

Pembroke Road was totally empty, the trees on either side still gently dripping water from the night's rain. The car was parked by the church, and my hand shook from the morning chill as I tried to open the door of the Rolls.

It was a Corniche—not bad for a working-class lad from Chelmsford, England, who had never finished school. We had bought it a year ago when David turned forty; a young age to own such an expensive, glittering machine. Now, it felt as lonely as an ice palace.

Eighteen years and four months ago we met in Tiffany's, the dance hall on Shaftesbury Avenue. I was a virginal, middle-class, intellectually snobbish twenty-year-old spending her first year in London after a cosseted upbringing in expensive schools. There were six of us that evening—Marion Keating was one of the girls, I wonder if she remembers—and we had spent it drinking in the Soho pubs and peeking into the strip clubs and giggling at the prostitutes soliciting up and down Wardour and Greek streets. It was all childishly exhilarating, and Tiffany's was to be our last stop for the evening.

It was, at the time, a large garish ballroom. The meeting place for secretaries and factory lads whose pockets were flush with money, and you danced to an eighteen-piece band under a revolving globe. Awful and tasteless, but we wanted to see how "ordinary" people spent their Saturday nights, to rub shoulders with them before returning to the sanctuary of art college.

We were sipping our sherries and sneering at girls' bouffant hairdo's and sharp boys' suits when I felt my arm touched. I turned.

A man was standing beside me. He did nothing for a moment except study me quietly. I sensed that he'd reached an important decision and was just savoring it. I glared at him, liking neither his hair style and well-cut suit, nor his confidence. He only smiled as if I'd confirmed his opinion.

"I fancy you, luv. Come and dance."

I was pushed from behind—by June Thornfield—and onto the floor with him while still shaking my head. We danced in silence for a moment. Then, having been brought up to make polite conversation whatever the situation or whoever the person, I did.

"Do you say that to every girl you meet?"

He tilted his head, listening. I wasn't sure whether to the music or to me. His hand gently pushed me in; I, just as gently, pushed out.

"Slumming?" His eyes were all lashes and eyebrows and missed little.

"Nothing of the sort."

I turned to look for the others, though I could feel his hand still pressing.

"I bet you come here every day, me little darling." His voice in my right ear was soft but brutal. "After eight hours bent over a typewriter . . . or would you be a factory bird? Yes, that's it. I can see you at a bench wiring radios, and all you're dreaming about is coming here to dance in your pretty red shoes."

"I came here to dance, not to discuss my employment situation. I don't, in fact, happen to work in a factory. If you must know."

He took my hand and, without looking, ran his thumb over the palm. The gesture felt surprisingly gentle.

Then he yanked my arm.

"You want to slum, come with me."

The heel of my shoe snapped off, and I nearly tripped. He had a hard hold on my hand and he was dragging me across the vast floor, pushing me through couples. I half hobbled, pulling back, then skidded and sailed past June and my other friends. He saw me looking at them, bewildered.

"Going to scream for help?"

I stood the best I could, one foot dangling.

"I am a woman who never screams."

"One day I'll make you." And we were off again.

I was out in the cool night. Shaftesbury Avenue was nearly deserted; the theater lights were all off. The street glistened at one end, near Piccadilly, and was dark at the other.

"I want to get my coat."

My back and half my chest were bare. He took off his jacket and tossed it around my shoulders. I was used to men holding open my coat.

We reached his car, an ancient MG, carefully polished so that it gleamed despite the rain and the misty street lights. For some reason that I didn't want to understand, I stood and waited while he got in and opened the door from the inside. I climbed in and slammed it hard.

"Why are you angry with me?" I asked.

"I'm not." The grin transformed his face. "That dance hall's just the tinsel, luv. You want to see slums, I'll take you to them. I'll be your guide. Free of charge."

I watched him out of the corner of my eye as he drove. He was young, in his early twenties; his face was strong and the fleshy nose not quite imperial. His eyes were narrowed to peer through the drizzle.

I don't know where we drove. I glimpsed the river and then we were south of it. He stopped the car as suddenly as he'd started. I looked out, recognizing nothing. I could have been on the moon.

He got out and waited for me. There were only one or two street lights on, the buildings narrow, mean and unlit. Some even looked broken and empty. The drizzle was heavier, the smell of the street rank. We walked in silence. A few windows were lit, yellowy, the movements behind them only dull silhouettes. There were abandoned spaces between some houses, and garbage and broken glass underfoot.

"Do you live . . . here?"

He shrugged: "You could say that. It's all the bloody same."

He stopped and we looked back. It seemed as if we'd walked down a tunnel, creepy and damp.

"I've left wherever I've come from. I'm going to be a millionaire by forty."

I'd never met anyone like him. In my small, pleasant world the men were polite. They only lived not to displease me. He had no resemblance to them.

"How?"

It was a stall. I had felt him studying me. I wasn't afraid, only nervous. The buildings around us were becoming grimmer as I hobbled and he walked.

"I have my own factory . . ." He hesitated and laughed. "Well, it's a workshop now but one day it'll be a factory. I and a mate make toys and games, and we also do our own marketing. It's tough at the moment, but we'll get there. I know we will."

"Are you always so sure?"

"Yes. I'm not going to be like me dad and granddad working all their fucking lives in a factory for someone else. I'm going to have my own."

He was fierce to look at in the shadows, and yet that desperate wanting to escape the past made him so vulnerable that I began to like him.

"Why did you ask me to dance?"

"Your eyes. I've never seen such green."

"You were too far away."

"We were a foot apart near the bar. You never saw me." He peered. "They look almost gray now."

I stepped back.

"I don't know your name!"

"Proper little lady, aren't you?"

He laughed, not at me, but at the sudden remembering, after nearly an hour of this stiff formality.

"David." And he put out his hand.

I took it, shy. It wasn't soft or calloused; just firm and dry.

"Shelley." Letting him keep hold.

He led me, gently, toward an abandoned, decaying house.

"I'm going to have you . . ."

"What?"

I dug in my one heel.

". . . for a wife."

I laughed, unsure.

"What would you have done if you hadn't seen me? Used the line on another bird?"

"No." He let go of my hand.

I could have escaped. I felt his mouth, soft, silken, just touch my lips. That first kiss, if it was that, lasted minutes. I felt no taking, only his asking. Then his mouth moved to my ear.

"I would have found you. I've been looking for you a long time."

He took my hand again and we were inside the house. He lit a match. Shadows leaped, fluttered, died. The darkness was even blacker, but he'd seen enough to lead the way, carefully, to the back.

He dropped his coat to the floor, spread it, knelt, took my hand, and pulled me slowly down. The smells were real: dust and brick and rain and, faintly, urine.

"I'm a virgin." My last defense as I lay back.

"There've been no virgins for three thousand years, luv."

It was as if we'd made love countless times before; except for the twinges and the faint blood on the lining of his jacket. He was gentle but firm. My bra unclipped with one movement, my garter belt with another. He stroked, kissed, murmured. I touched him, rock-hard and magnificent, and helped, desperately needing him in me. The floor beneath me, harsh and unforgiving . . . above me his pale, shadowy face. I kissed it. He became fierce gradually and I with him.

Oh god, it was all a dream which remained even when we just lay next to each other on the cold floor. There was a three-inch bruise in the small of my back the next morning.

"Are you really going to marry me?"

"Yes."

"Why?"

"I told you."

"Tell me more."

"Well, if I took out a bird from my own class, married her and had kids, by the time I reached forty, and rich, I'd divorce her and marry someone like you." My eyes were wide and staring. "You see, she wouldn't be able to keep up with me and one day she'd find I'd left her behind. So . . . I need someone who'll keep up with me."

I was his fantasy: birth, breeding, and beauty. Though so English, I looked Mediterranean with my shoulder-length dark hair, ever-changing hazel eyes, high cheekbones and a wide mouth. I wasn't voluptuous; my breasts were the size of his cupped palms, and my legs were long and slim.

"And how many children am I to produce?"

"Three." Completely missing the sarcasm.

"And what happens if, at this magical age of forty, you decide I'm not good enough for your dreams? Divorce me?"

"I won't."

He didn't. He just disappeared with a female. Maybe she is an aristocrat, a princess of royal and ancient blood, possibly even a Rockefeller or a Rothschild, who will keep pace with his ambition.

Worse: she could be a child with a young fresh body and manipulative limbs.

I must have sat and stared at the house for half an hour before I realized where I was. Dear thing! Glass and mortar and brick and wood, lawns and beech trees, all smug and pretty in the moonlight. I felt like one of those snails whose shell had been stolen for making escargots. I can crawl back in, but the feeling is no longer the same. The pain embedded in the house will make it too difficult to be comfortable.

The house was quiet. None of the children would be awake: there were still hours of privacy to be had. It was the holidays, and I allowed them to sleep as late as they wanted. The rooms were cool and smelt as if they too slept. The air was still and there wasn't a sound as I moved from room to room, aimlessly touching things.

At one in the morning in a strange room, it was easy to decide to get David back. I hadn't the faintest idea how, I didn't know where he was; his letter only had a date, and the stamp a Heathrow Airport cancellation. I didn't doubt I wanted him back.

It was love, but not that alone. In time the intensity of loving, liking, affection—even at times despairing and hating—might have eased and slipped into indifference. I didn't want that indifference, nor did I want another to replace him. He was my habit, my comfort, my dear, dear friend. We had grown together, one into the other like trees trapped in a jungle: our thoughts, our feelings, our tastes were intertwined. He was tearing himself out and I would have to hack at myself to free him. And I wanted him back for the purely selfish reason that I'd planned that we grow old together, die together, be buried together.

He had said eighteen years ago that he wanted me as his wife. Now I wanted him with the same egotistical force with which he'd claimed me. I had no intention of being discarded like some working-class bird.

Our bedroom looked untenanted. The walnut double bed with the lavender coverlet undisturbed seemed vast. My dressing table was cluttered; his was almost bare, covered with a sheen of dust thick enough for me to write his name in it. On his bedside table was *The*

Honourable Schoolboy; on mine, unread, *Supernature*. It was impossible to read so alone.

I undressed and ran the bath. The walls were wood and painted amber, and by the tub was a floor-to-ceiling mirror. David had installed a shower after he'd begun to visit the States. I never used it; I was raised to soak in warm, perfumed baths. His electric razor was still in the cabinet. I hoped he wasn't using an ordinary razor, as he always cut himself. The electric had been one of my Christmas presents.

I took his letter, tightly balled, from the drawer. I would have shredded it, but I'd known that one day I would want to relive the pain. I'd read it only once, hurriedly. It had been like looking at one's death sentence, and there was no need to read the commas to feel the savage stab of the words.

Dear Shelley

(In eighteen years had I drained him so much that he couldn't use the dearest, the darling? It was the formality that had frightened me.)

I am very sad to be writing this. It was something that I had never planned to do, and tried everything possible to avoid it. I have fallen in love with someone, you don't know her, and am in the States hoping to start a new life with her. I wish I could explain how and why it happened, but as you know I just don't have the words. The past 18 years have been very happy ones for me, and I hope for you. You were the most important person to have entered my life, and if this hadn't happened we would have had eighteen more and another eighteen after that.

I also feel the pain of leaving the children. They are so, so dear to me. At some time I will try to tell them why I left, if I ever understand. In the meantime I know you will explain without needing to destroy me in their eyes. You're not that kind of woman.

I hope you will be able to forgive me for the mess I've left but you're a strong woman and I know you'll cope.

Love ... David!

I suddenly felt chilled. I hadn't read the last sentence before—I'd crumpled the letter at "children." Mess? I knew David well enough to know that he meant something more than just his leaving.

CHAPTER 2

I WAS DRESSED MY BEST, IN A LEMON SHANTUNG SUIT, on Monday morning. I had washed and set my hair carefully and spent nearly two hours on my face and selecting my outfit and accessories. I carried the handbag that David had brought me a year ago from Rome. It wasn't my favorite, but expensive and beautiful. The careful exterior of silks and perfumes camouflaged my queasy interior. Nothing that happened in the bank would shake the facade of serenity.

I slid the car into the only vacant space opposite the bank of St. James's Square, just beating out a dreadful red sports car. He "varoomed" in frustration as I got out.

Berman's, on the corner next to the London Library, had only half a dozen branches in the country. David loved its granite archway and heavy oak door, the porter standing by to heave it open and shut. The popular banks with their countless branches reminded him of a supermarket chain.

The square was busy, and as I walked I could feel the long glances of the hurrying men and women. Each look caressed me pleasantly. By the time Charlie pulled open the door, I had enough confidence to face a firing squad.

Nothing ever changed in Berman's. The carpets were forever the same dark green, the doors warm and polished, the glasses frosted, the air washed with silences. I didn't touch the brass-plaqued doors. They were opened for me, one after another, down the long corridors. It was a regal passage that momentarily faltered at the "Customers' Accounts" doorway. That one was opened too. I smiled and swept in.

Mr. Samuels, tall and stooped, came from behind his desk to pull up a chair. I sat, smiled, waited. He wanted to know what the weather was doing outside. I had no idea. It obviously wasn't raining, as I was dry.

He flattened the papers in front of him with a dry, crisp hand. "It's going to rain later. Showers, the forecast said."

A child could have predicted rain. Genius predicted sun.

"Have you checked our accounts, Mr. Samuels?"

"Yes, Mrs. Warwick."

I sensed the menace of those papers as he said it; his liquid gray eyes were worried and full of mute apology. He fumbled and coughed.

"Tell me briefly ... please."

"I don't quite understand what Mr. Warwick has done. Over the last three months he has drawn large sums of money, which is rather unusual for him. You see ..."

"What is left?"

He blinked and his eyes slid to a point over my left shoulder.

"Nothing."

"Nothing?"

"An overdraft, I'm afraid." He glanced down at the papers and shuffled them. "He drew out a hundred thousand pounds in three months. I had advised him against liquidity but he wouldn't listen."

"Shares, investments . . ." My financial knowledge came to a halt.

"Cashed. He said he needed the capital for some . . . ah . . . other investments."

"When did he cash them?"

"Over three months ago." Poring over his papers like a priest over sacred papyrus. "March fifteenth . . . twenty-five thousand . . . March thirtieth . . . twelve thousand . . ."

I couldn't listen. My hand shook as I lit a cigarette and nearly singed an eyelash. Three months and a hundred thousand pounds? David was generous but not stupid with money. He would not have forgotten the children or me. To have drawn that amount meant either a madness in love or just plain madness.

I dismissed my ignorance of his love affair with a puff of smoke blown over Mr. Samuel's papers. I wasn't a woman who picked hairs off a husband's coat or sniffed to detect an alien perfume. Deception was easy in a marriage. It only takes a couple of hours to fuck, and no trace need ever be left.

There had been three or four—the figure could have been higher—pieces on the side for David. A buyer at a department store, an actress, a model. The first one had hurt, but essentially these encounters had made no difference to us. David could have women when he wanted, but by the second time in bed, they bored him. Just as the two men I'd had—a racing driver one summer, and before him a poet who only drank like Dylan Thomas—failed to interest me after one weekend. We could have both affaired ourselves to death, but those bodies were, instead, brief diversions.

Mr. Samuels coughed. The recitation of dates was over. His curiosity hovered between those papers and my décolletage. A flicker of lust, rusty with disuse, brought color to his face. He settled, embarrassed, for the papers.

"Has Mr. Warwick invested in . . . ah . . . what he intended?"

"Naturally."

"Possibly he could come in one day soon and settle the matter. As I said, I've written . . ."

"He's away just now. He'll be back in a month."

I rose. I would bring him back.

"I'd like to take something from our safe deposit box."

He took my key. It was damp with perspiration. I had clutched it so hard that the imprint was in the palm. David also had a key.

Mr. Samuels walked ahead, opening doors, muttering about the weather. If he were a plant or a tree I could understand his obsession. Such an awful British habit.

The old lift, mirrored and gilt edged, took us down a floor. Mr. Wilson, even more ancient and fragile than Mr. Samuels, slid open the book. I signed and was about to return it.

"Excuse me."

I flicked back the pages. One month, six weeks, seven. I nearly screamed when I saw David's sprawling signature.

"Here you are."

The deposit room was cool, morgueish. White-walled, gray-boxed, green-carpeted. The decor made me feel ill. Mr. Samuels opened one lock, Mr. Wilson the other. Reverently they slid out the box, presented it to me and withdrew. I chose a cubicle and sat without moving for a moment. Was the facade cracking? I checked my mirror: no visible signs of an impending collapse. I pulled out my list of contents and laid it next to the box.

A futile gesture. The diamond necklace, diamond ring, two emerald bracelets, emerald earrings, topaz choker and two thousand ICI shares were gone. David was honorable. He had taken only what was his. The jewels had been his gifts: the necklace for the birth of Miranda, the choker on our tenth anniversary, the bracelet bought in Beirut for no other reason than that we were happy ...

He had left what I needed. The deed to the house. I unfolded the papers. He had signed it over to me two months ago. I refolded them hurriedly; I hadn't been told. I opened the box: lying snugly in their velvet beds were the coins, willed to me by Uncle Cecil. They looked dull and worn, heavy with lead, gold and history. I kept them for the children and, once a year, ascertained their value from Arthur Horden, the numismatist under the Charing Cross Bridge. In February, he had totaled their worth and whistled. The whistle was worth one hundred thousand pounds. I dropped them into my purse, threw the papers back into the box and closed it.

Mr. Samuels escorted me as far as the pavement.

"As soon as Mr. Warwick returns I trust he'll settle the matter satisfactorily."

"You make it sound like a duel."

"Not quite. Good-bye, Mrs. Warwick."

When I started off, he was still standing, watching. I had one more stop to make before home. Now that I knew the worst I felt a little better.

Sunday had been tense, and I, awful. I prowled the house full of worry and pain; the children sensed my mood and stayed clear. Charles, after his morning football game, had remained in his room, and the two girls had played as quietly as angels. I stood for what seemed like hours staring at the roll-top desk in David's study. There were secrets in it I had never wanted to see. David had the only key, and it was so beautiful that I didn't want to break into it. I'd decided to postpone the event until visiting the bank.

The Chelmsford Toy Company was on St. John's Road. From a small room in the East End it had grown to a factory in Ilford and then a heavy brass plaque outside a two-story building in London. The office took up the whole top floor. I had done the decorating: light and airy, off-white walls, trailing plants and prints on the walls.

There was a new secretary outside David's office.

"Where's Mrs. Clayton?"

The girl's blank look suited her personality. I repeated the question, she repeated the expression. I walked past her to the door.

"I presume Mike is in."

"Do you have an appointment?"

"Don't be silly."

She was reaching for the phone when I entered. The office hadn't changed except for the man behind the desk. Mike Pierce, as David's partner, would have been sitting in the office across the hall. He was a tall man with crooked teeth and a neatly trimmed beard. I had always liked him.

"Shelley, you look beautiful. Ravishing, in fact."

I liked him. He was always truthful, no matter how I looked. We embraced. His warmth and familiar smell nearly made me cry. The face and room shimmered, then cleared. Mike didn't notice.

"It's been some time, Shelley. Three months? We used to see so much of each other in the beginning. How are you? How's David?"

That shook me. He was watching with friendly curiosity.

"He's left me."

It took him moments.

"I'm . . . I'm sorry. I didn't know."

I wonder if it's the inadequacy of our language. Everyone said the same "I'm sorry," as if it were they who had caused me the pain.

"I thought you knew."

I gestured. Looking around, I noticed another

change. A small painting, a self-portrait I'd done in college, was missing.

"I didn't. Six weeks ago David resigned. He said he wanted to do something new, stretch himself, he said. He still has shares in the company but . . . when did he leave?"

"Six weeks ago. He left a note, that's all."

"Honestly, I didn't know. He's a stupid bastard to have left someone as smashing as you." He came around the desk, worry in every fold of his face. "Is there anything you need?"

I shook my head. I *would not* burst into tears.

"Where's Mrs. Clayton?"

"When David left, she did as well."

We smiled. It would have been neat: David and Mrs. Clayton. She was fifty and had been with him for years. Her husband was a cricket fanatic and she spent every Saturday scoring for his team.

Mike walked me to the car, patting my back awkwardly the way my father did when he wanted to convey affection.

"Did you know of any girl? And please, Mike, don't try to hide anything from me."

"No." His eyes remained steady. "You know as well as I do David had one or two on the side, but they were never important. You were everything."

"Until now." A traffic warden began to stalk the car. "I'm going to get him back. When we first met he knew what I should do with my life. Now, I know what to do with his."

"Any idea who she is?"

"Not yet."

"Best of luck, Shelley."

"I'm going to need more than that."

We kissed and I got into the car. A childish impulse. I stuck my tongue out at the warden as I pulled away. It was better than screaming.

At sixteen, two years before leaving the convent boarding school in Dorset, I had yearned for sainthood. Having passed the awesome discovery of maturity by two years, I was still unaware of my sensuality. The body was still undeveloped, like a pasture before spring and after a very long winter. I was dismayed and frightened with the talk of sex; giggly innuendos only, for we were all ignorant, having been neither voyeurs nor, as I thought then, victims.

When I heard the girls talking I knew that I would be incapable of such awful physical passion, of this lust that would drive me insane. God, I decided, would grant me immunity. My favorite teacher was Sister Bianca; the picture has faded but I remember her as beautiful, compassionate and gentle. Her only passion was for God, and in that sixteenth year I vowed that I would grow up to be Sister Shelley: untouched by man, healing lepers in the dark corners of the world, serving and suffering passionately, beautifully.

One winter evening, I confided my ambition to Sister Bianca. She smiled, having heard a thousand girls pledging their escape from a soiled world. "When you've finished school, we'll talk more about it," she said in her sweet English lisp. By summer I had abandoned the dream, having fallen madly in love with a captain in Father's command who only gently returned it. Yet I never quite forgot that brief and exhilarating sense of purity.

In the third year of our marriage, I regained it. Charles, a difficult birth, was just two months old. I, exhausted and sore, couldn't make love—though savegely wanting to. David was patient, but I suppose with men the erection, whatever the cost, cannot be denied.

It had drizzled until six that autumn day, and then brightened. The light outside the drawing room window was soft and lingering, like a Turner painting. The world as far as I could see—the sky, the trees, the grass—seemed to glow. I commanded it to remain that way, a feast, until David returned from work so that he too could see it. It made an effort to obey: I sat for hours watching until streaks of gray began to spread through the whole canvas, darkening it gently, almost reluctantly; until it had enveloped the whole landscape, leaving me alone with a sleepless child.

I was, for an hour in the darkness, not human, not cerebral or physical, only a spirit fragile with beauty and love. Had David come then he would have glimpsed not just my heart but my whole being. I felt liquid; ready to pour myself over him, supplicate him with my hair, my eyes, my mouth, my hands.

He came in at three that morning. The liquid by then had turned to rage. He was wet with rain that had begun around midnight, his belly was swollen with beer, and his face and body smelled of Tweed perfume. "I'm sorry," countless times, cradling, kissing, touching me. He wanted forgiveness but it was beyond me even if I had wanted to give it. I was too angry.

"Don't touch me," whipping him in return—not so much for the pain he had caused as for the love he'd missed.

The next morning I took Charles, packed a case, and entered the convent in Hertfordshire where Sister Bianca had moved. David came on my second day—I thought him clever to have found me so easily. It was only much later that I learned Sister Bianca had phoned him and found him frantic after having checked mother, uncles, aunts and countless friends.

I refused to see him. I should have expected it: he refused to leave the convent or to touch any food, bewildering the poor nuns who were used to dealing with an amiable God and tractable young women. For two days and nights David and I held our respective positions like stalemated armies. My capitulation, when it finally came, wasn't a humble one. I sailed past him—sitting dejected in the hall—with Charles in my arms. I felt that the interlude of piety had done both of us some good.

"I've got the car." A secondhand Ford, battered and comfortable. David, contrite, helpless to my whims, kept pace with me.

"And I've got a taxi." I got in and slammed the door. "You may follow."

The fare would be enough to humble any man. I forgave him when I felt it was high enough and dismissed the taxi at a traffic light as he pulled up for the umpteenth time by my window to plead his cause.

"I've forgotten what happened last week, David." He scrambled around the car, traffic piling up behind us, to open the door. "Next time make it less obvious."

It was delivered not as a plea but as a demand, and he obeyed it.

Mrs. Clayton lived on the sixth floor and as I climbed I prayed she was in. I was panting by the time I reached her floor. I leaned against the cool wall. If I were a man I'd promise myself a daily run around the common. David always did. I only swore I'd never attempt another long climb.

Mrs. Clayton—cheerful, gray-haired, stubby, and always effusive—was in. As she clasped me, hard, I hoped she wasn't going to be as ignorant of the whole thing as Mike had been. The flat was too colorfully decorated. There was too much blue and the prints were of rearing horses.

"Tea or coffee?"

"Vodka. Straight." She glanced at the clock. It was only noon. "Please."

Mrs. Clayton handed me the glasss. "How are the children?"

"Where's David?"

I had to get to the point. Her politeness would have kept her prattling on about the children. She had none and I knew it hurt.

"Oh dear!" She didn't look happy with the question.

She was about to repeat herself when she caught my eye over the rim of the vodka glass and stopped. Her hesitation was, I suspected, in defense of David. She had been with him twelve years and her love for him, though not the same as mine, wanted to blame me. Women are not the same pack animals as men.

"I don't know. It seems so odd that he should have . . . left . . . you and the children."

"I'm trying to find out why. And get him back."

She clasped her hands. "How marvelous. I was telling my Jimmy that you both were such a happy couple and he said . . ."

"What was David like before he left?"

"Restless. He didn't seem sure what he wanted to do. Mind you, it's only my opinion but I had the feeling he really didn't want to do it. The 'it' meaning leaving you. At the time I didn't know, of course."

Restless? A peculiar word for David. He was never restless. He was calm and thoughtful. It took him very little time to make a decision and once he did, he stuck to it. Somehow, I would have to unstick him.

"I never noticed it."

"Neither did I until he snapped at me. Mr. Warwick never snapped. It was about a call I took from a girl. I can't remember her name."

"Try. You've got to."

"I can't. It was a funny name. She wanted to speak to him and I wouldn't put her through until she told me her business. She refused. It's my business to filter calls, otherwise you get people bothering him."

"Can't you remember anything about her?"

"She was American. I know that. I'd guess from Chicago."

"How do you know?"

"I spent a month there."

At the end of half an hour, she still couldn't remember the girl's name. She promised to phone me the moment she did.

It had begun to drizzle. Mr. Samuels would be dancing on his desk in ecstasy. The thought made me giggle. He was the kind of man, and I imagined them to be in the millions, who would ejaculate only dust from his dry body.

At home, I changed into jeans and a pullover, then went to the desk. The mahogany gleamed in the sunlight and when I bent over it and sniffed, I smelt the wax I'd lavished so often on the wood. I gripped the screwdriver and pushed it into the lock. It slid and scratched the wood.

"Charles!"

A grumble from his room. He came down at the second shout, wilted and crumpled from his doze. Or from doing whatever boys do in the privacy of their rooms.

"Break."

I pointed and handed him the screwdriver. He was a modern child who understood gestures rather than sentences. At fifteen he was a professional. He studied the lock, contemptuously returned the tool and fetched another. Three years of expensive schooling had given him a certainty about locks, if nothing else. He raised an eyebrow to confirm that the order was genuine and snapped the lock with one blow.

"Thank you, Charles. I can take it from here."

"Dad won't like it." Curiosity stalled him.

"I promise not to tell him you broke it."

I pushed him out of the door. I needed to be alone to bear whatever was to be found.

"You told me to break it."

"I did, but if you ask for it in writing I'll scream. Now go back to whatever you were doing."

The desk slid, stuck, slid. I was perspiring, not from exertion but from expectation, by the time I had it rolled all the way up. David was neat. The pigeonholes were neatly labeled: tax, household, children, Shelley.

Five years ago, indignant, I had asked to be de-slotted but David gently insisted that this was his way of keeping track of my expenses. I rifled through the Shelley papers. There certainly were not enough bills to send a man off. The left-hand drawers held business papers, but I went through them carefully nonetheless.

I stopped. There were two Tunisian airline-ticket folders. I opened them. The carbons showed they were to Djerba. I had never been there nor, to my knowledge, had David. The first was his; the other was for a Ms. C. Schraft.

I had been hunched over the desk; my back hurt when I straightened up. Schraft, C. Dated January 20. C.? Cathy? Caroline? Cunt?

The tickets lay like wounds in the palms of my hands. They held secrets: his passion, her attraction, written by a stranger. I dropped them on the floor.

I returned to the desk with a bottle of vodka and a glass. My face was no longer my protection. It felt scorched with pain as I touched the lines under the eyes and around the mouth. To my sensitive fingers, they felt deeper and very recent. I had no more curiosity for the desk, only fear. There could be other pieces of paper hidden inside and each would become another wound. By the time I finished, I'd be lying around the floor like so many slices of bacon; cured in vodka, naturally.

At our beginning, David had only known of Presley. Now he knew Puccini, Pollack, Pinter and—I peered at the transparent charge receipt—Kutchinsky. One clover-shaped gold pendant, insert with diamonds, nine hundred pounds. The need to visualize this C. who wore a Kutchinsky gold clover was too much. I needed to feed on more than her last name and initial. I rang the jewelers.

"Hello, this is Mrs. Warwick. A couple of months ago I bought a clover-shaped gold pendant, inset with diamonds. Could I talk to the gentleman who sold it to us?"

A man finally came on the line.

"Are you the sweet gentleman who sold us the pendant?"

"Yes, Mrs. Warwick. I remember you."

"I bet you don't."

"I certainly do."

"All right, describe me."

"You're a very pretty blonde, not too tall, blue eyes, around twenty-four . . ."

She materialized: luminescent, beautiful, shinily new, like a goddess out of flames. As she rose, she held my David between her teeth.

". . . American . . ." He trailed off.

"You really do remem-bah." It may have been southern, western, or Californian, I couldn't care less. "I'll drop in tomorrow and pick up another. Thank you."

I sat down carefully, though I really wanted to crumple. The vodka was having no effect. I could have poured a cask of it down my throat and remained sober.

I was trembling with hesitation, doubt, pity, determination, bloody rage. The vibrations were fierce and rapid; I felt them all with an energy that exhausted me. The decision made in a strange room evaporated once again. He had abandoned me, now I wanted to abandon him. I couldn't.

And David?

I heard the back door slam. Samantha and Miranda, rosy and so beautiful, were trailing Sammy, the spaniel pup, as they bounced into the room.

I had them bathed and ready for bed by seven o'clock. As I hugged them and led them down for dinner I could smell the innocent odors of their bodies. They were so vulnerable to everything that would happen to me from now on. If I succeeded, they would lead normal lives, if I didn't, they would grow somewhat askew. Whatever happened, I would never use them to lever David's return.

"I didn't tell you all the truth." Three faces peered up from their plates. "Your father didn't go away on a business trip. He left us."

"I know." Charles sounded smug.

"You did. Your sisters didn't. I'm taking you all to stay with Granddad and Grandmother. I am going to get your father back."

"Suppose he doesn't want to come back?" Samantha, at ten, asked the question.

"He will." I had to make myself believe.

"If he left us, does that mean he doesn't want us?" Miranda wobbled on the edge of sobs.

"Of course he wants us. At times, in a marriage, because we grow so used to it, we forget what we have. Love, and needs, and responsibilities. We look at someone else and we're suddenly excited by that person and we want to escape what we have. But it's only that—an escape."

We women, huddled around the dining table, were ready to fall into each other's arms and cry our eyes out. Charles was watching skeptically.

"Most of my friends' parents at school are divorced." Solemnly, he ticked them off. "Dick's, Tony's, Roger's. Norman's are separated. Derek's mother is having it off with an actor . . . so he says." He studied me very carefully. "You're not too bad. I mean for your age. I'm sure there'll be someone who'll fancy you."

"Thank you, Charles. I don't want someone else. I want your father."

They brooded over the news. The phone began to ring when Charles decided to speak. I beat him to it. "This family is not a democracy, Charles. It is a dictatorship. There is no freedom of speech, movement or thought until you reach eighteen. Now answer the phone."

He got up and trotted out. Act as a mother and he balks; behave as a senior prefect and he snaps to attention. The girls were grinning.

"This dictatorship applies to you two as well. When I leave you at Granddad's, if I hear of any naughtiness while I'm gone . . ."

Charles returned to the table. He said nothing; just took his seat.

"All right. Who was that?"

"Dad. He wants to talk to you."

CHAPTER

3

"OH MY GOD. WHAT ABOUT?"

"He didn't say. He asked me how I was. I said . . . I said I missed him." He was near to tears.

I would have cradled Charles against me, but he wanted to be brave. He allowed me to tousle his head as I went out and closed the door.

At the beginning when you are in love—and lust and need and touch—just his presence, even so distant and disembodied, is enough to make you start to come. I was shaking, wet and ready to be fucked. It was not years but centuries since I had felt this: an exuberant, terrifying new womanhood, five years or so before menopause.

I sat down on the Victorian chair and picked up the phone.

"Hello, David."

If only I could have poured myself down the instrument. Words would never ever be enough for our needs, they translate so little of what we feel. We should have replaced them with those guttural, longing sounds animals make in a jungle at night.

"Hello, Shelley. How are you?"

There were plenty of answers. "I love you," "I'm feeling rotten," "I miss you," "I'm coming after you." None would do.

"Fine."

"Oh."

"You did tell me I was a strong woman."

"Yes, I did. Shelley, I'm sorry about everything."

"So am I. Where are you?"

"America."

"I know *that*. Where in America?"

"I won't tell you, Shelley."

I waited, sensing he wanted something. Me?

"I need some money, Shelley."

"You've got it all, silly."

"The coins."

"You can't have them."

"I've got to close a deal and haven't the capital. I *need* them, Shelley."

"I don't know."

"Please, Shelley, you'll get them back in a month."

"Well . . ."

"Give them to Burt Mellows. He's staying at the Connaught."

"Who's he?"

"A business partner."

"You certainly move fast."

"You know I always have. Get them to him today. Please. I swear I'll return the money. How are the children?"

"Fine. They miss you."

"Tell them I love them."

"Why don't you do that yourself?"

"I'd . . . rather not upset them. Good-bye, Shelley."

"Damn, damn, damn."

The children came running out of the dining room as I slammed the phone down on the fragile table. It tottered and fell over. I had the strength to crush it to matchsticks with my hands. Instead I kicked, forgetting

I was wearing slippers. I grabbed my injured foot and let out an aria of screams. The physical pain, combined with my anger at David and at myself, was too much. I screamed, hopped, screamed. The children ducked back into the dining room and shut the door on me.

I picked up the Dresden boatman we'd found in Dublin, drew my hand and aimed at the small gold-framed Matisse. It was a thirty-second birthday present from David. I held the pose.

Sanity, the part of me that was captivated by the beauty of all these objects, held back my hand. It wanted me to preserve this mausoleum of culture and civilization, built by breeding, education and carefully cultivated taste: this fucking tomb filled with dead air. I should have built my world with the crap spilled from a madman, gargoyles fused out of iron by demented dwarfs.

I threw the boatman. It hit the edge of the Matisse, cracking the glass into glittering white fragments. Released, I picked up the table and hurled it through the late-nineteenth-century glass mahogany cabinet. I couldn't rip the silk cushion; my fingers slid helplessly over the fabric. I threw the stereo against the wall. I didn't know whether it broke or not: it must have. I stamped and kicked and smashed and tore.

By the time I collapsed on the floor, pleasurably exhausted, the room was wrecked. I sat, letting my breath return, then got up and went out.

The girls had shiny streaks down their cheeks. Charles had moved near them. I had no doubt that without him they'd still be bawling.

"Are you angry with us, Mummy?" Miranda started to sniffle.

"No, my darlings. I just felt like that."

"Feeling better?"

I smiled at Charles's concern. "A bit. Dad also asked me how you were, and said to tell you he loves you."

"What did you tell him? About how we are."

"That you miss him. That we all do."

"Well, I tried to be brave on the phone."

"So did I. I hope you didn't tell him what I was going to do."

Charles grinned. "No. Let him find out for himself. He needs the shock." He played with his dessert spoon for a few moments. "I'm so mad at him for having left us." Charles smiled. "If I thought I could have gotten away with it, I'd have done what you just did."

"One wrecked room is enough for tonight, Charles."

"It's going to cost us a fortune."

"I'll worry about that later."

Charles stood up and at attention. "Any edicts to be issued before I go up to my room?"

"Yes. You will pack your things for the stay with Granddad and Grandmother. I'm going to drive up tomorrow morning after breakfast, so if you've made any plans cancel them. That's all I can think of for the moment. If anything else comes to mind I'll let you know."

They scrambled.

Charles saluted and wheeled out of the room.

"You two, also . . . Upstairs and get into bed. I'll come and kiss you good-night and do your packing after I wash up. Off, off."

They scrambled.

I lay on my bed, wearing nothing but the soft gauze of moonlight coming through the window. I looked down and wriggled my toes. The right foot throbbed a little. I flexed my knees, my fingers touched the thick pubic hairs, caressed the firm tight flesh around the belly, moving up to cradle my breasts. I felt warm, soft and alive. Breathing in the perfume I'd lavished on my skin, I folded my arms under my breasts, which meant lifting them just a little: in the half light, they looked high and firm, like a twenty-five-year-old's. I closed my eyes: there were times when I longed to rape my own body.

I had soaked for an hour in the bath after putting the girls to bed. Dried and scented and naked, I went down to the room. The rubble of broken things looked savage. There were bits and pieces of me in the cracked glass and shattered furniture. I felt no regret for the ruins as I tiptoed through, touching gravestones with my foot. I wanted to dance. Why not? I hesitated and then danced, humming.

I had danced as a child, not wildly or ungracefully, but with bloody ordered delicacy. My ambition had been to be another Fonteyn and daily, dutifully, I had disciplined my body. How I wished I had instead learned the mating dances of an orangutan and how to swing through the trees.

The bed, which had seemed so vast, now had returned to normal size. The empty space would be filled; it was a matter of time, thought and strategy. It was suprising that only a day ago I had felt lonely and shriveled lying in that bed.

A cloud was slowly drifting across the moon, and my body gradually faded before my eyes. I had a moment of unease. The coins! I would regret their loss, no longer because they were the heritage for my children but because we would need them ourselves when David returned. There had to be a way of keeping them. I shut my eyes; I wanted to recall every syllable and sound of our conversation, even the silences, for they spoke more to me than what he'd said. Silence, words, silence. The urgency of his commands returned. Well, I wasn't about to hurl them into unknown space. David's "business partner" at the Connaught would tell me nothing. Without the coins, I would never be able to find him.

The sun and the girls awoke me. They were lying on David's side of the bed, whispering to each other. They fell silent the moment I opened my eyes. I felt the same calm as I had the night before. While they watched and we talked, I exercised exuberantly, feeling the muscles tighten, the flesh glow pink and firm enough if not to match a twenty-five-year-old's then enough to hold my own.

"Will Daddy come back with you?" Miranda asked.

"Yes." I touched my toes ten times.

"Why did he leave? Was it because we'd done something?"

"No, darlings, it wasn't what you'd done. Me and Daddy. We both forgot why we married, why we loved, we both just forgot. It happens. We start getting concerned with things that just aren't important and we build shelter to hide in."

"From who, Mummy?"

"From ourselves. From each other."

I swung from side to side at the hips; my breasts could never keep time and I was reminded of a stripper I once saw in Beirut. She could whirl her breasts and, though I laughed, there had been a moment of envy.

"Right now, I'm feeling it's all my fault that your father left because I don't have him here to tell me why he did it. It could also be his fault. I'll find out when I see him."

"You won't be away long, will you?" Samantha asked. "I'll miss you, like I miss Daddy."

"I don't know how long, but I'll miss you all and I know Daddy does as well. He said so."

We were out of the house an hour behind schedule. Charles was helpful and surprisingly obedient. He took the back seat, allowing the girls to sit up front with me.

"If Dad doesn't come back, what'll we do?"

One day, he would look like David. He was now a few inches shorter than his father, and thinner. Given a few years he would fill out and up. He had the same strong mouth and if he didn't insist on wearing his hair so long, the rest of his face would match its strength.

The eyebrows were a shade sparser; the eyes, however, were steady. They didn't slide away, shy and nervous; they held and bored in. I hadn't noticed: he had, before, been only my son. He would take women the way his father had.

"He will come back."

"But have you thought about what if he doesn't?"

It would be the loneliness that would frighten me the most, as it had these past two months. The terror of losing and staying lost in a world which had once been warm with companionship. Yet nothing is eternal. In time the man, like the pain, would fade even though his children remained as reminders.

"What would you suggest?"

Charles frowned, obviously having given the matter some thought.

"You could take a job, but what would you do? Dad always said you were a scatterbrain about money, so you couldn't do business, could you?"

"I could hire an accountant if you have a good business idea." I took the ramp off the Edgware Road, pointed the car toward the A4 and Oxford, and slid into the fast lane.

"You could become Mike's partner or something."

"I'm not sure I'd like to step into Dad's shoes there." I glanced at the mirror. "How about my old job?"

"After sixteen *years*?"

"I suppose you're right, but I have kept in touch with the business. I could start in my old position and work my way up. It would have to be part time as long as Samantha and Miranda are young."

Samantha looked up at me seriously, and held my hand. "We'll promise not to be young too long."

"Take your time. If I were you, I'd stay young forever. It's a lot better than being grown up."

Charles considered my employment suggestions, none too pleased with them.

"There won't be enough money."

"Then we'd get rid of this car and move into a smaller house."

"I don't think I'd like that," said Miranda.

"Neither would I. Especially since your school's close by."

"What about mine?" Charles looked worried.

"I'd manage that, but you'd have to take a wage freeze. All of you, and that includes me as well."

That took care of the present and kept them occupied. A car, a house, a few dresses. All superficial and unnecessary and nothing to really hurt. The hurt would only come with the long, quiet tick of days and nights as they grew up, and I grew older.

"And what if I did marry again as suggested, Charles?"

A long silence. I caught glimpses of him as he shifted uneasily in his seat.

"I suppose . . . if you want. Though we three should be considered."

"I wouldn't have it otherwise."

We passed Uxbridge. The girls, worshipful of their elder brother, had actually remained quiet together in the front seat. By chance I looked up. Charles was studying my face. His eyes flicked away and his face pinked. It was amusing. He had been weighing me not as a son but as a man.

The look hadn't been Oedipal. Charles, so long a son, was giving me points the way other men do. My mouth, my eyes, my nose, and when we stopped to fill the tank I caught him studying my breasts, my legs and ass. The scales were being balanced: did he find me attractive? Would another man, if I didn't find David? What was my worth?

I turned just before we reached the M4. The traffic thinned and I slowed the car. It was a clear, sunny day, and as we moved farther from the main highway and into the narrower roads, flanked by hedged wheatfields and herds of cows, I felt at ease. I was returning home.

"Charles!" I watched him in the mirror. "Are you a virgin?"

He held my eyes, smiled secretively.

"What's virgin?" Samantha listened only to words which sounded interesting.

"Never mind."

"No," said Charles.

Somewhere, a girl, a woman—I hoped not a whore, for they are permanent strangers to men—had a memory of Charles inside her. I shouldn't have exulted; yet, peculiarly, we want our sons to be men. To have as many women as possible, by love, by lies, by force, though we ourselves do not want to be taken with the last two. Certainly I did not. Yet, even in giving myself, I felt at times that by David's penetration a rape had taken place. It is so impossible to love without being violated.

The first weekend David met my parents, I forced him to make love to me in my bed. It had, over a decade, been impregnated with my virtue; my schoolgirl's body had impressed its growing shape on the mattress—and no one had ever made another indentation on it. I wanted the memories of innocence and first menstrual blood to be massively destroyed by an act of violation. At first, within hearing distance of my parents, David balked. The working classes have such a marvelous sense of propriety. I didn't need to force him—I unzipped his fly. Men are too easy to rape.

Mother, still beautiful and commanding, was disdainful at their first meeting. She never changed; neither did David. Class, to mother—like the flag and the Queen—was only a thing worth dying for. She would never have minded being ravished by a count, but no Rockefeller might kiss her cheek. She was immune to charm, wealth and education; painfully vulnerable to breeding.

"What do you do?" Mother asked over cocktails.

"Work," David said cheerfully.

"Oh?"

An "Oh" from mother could fill three pages of the Oxford Dictionary with meaning.

"I mean I have my own firm, I'm going to be a millionaire by forty."

"Oh."

This time four pages.

Mother disapproved of commercial work. As the daughter of a general, married to a general—both of whom I think led the modern equivalent of the Charge of the Light Brigade in the Somme and Singapore and were knighted for their services—mother couldn't believe that people aspired to millionairedom. But it was also part veneer. I had, as a child, seen her hold a dying baby to her starched white blouse and wash its tiny body with her tears. It was done, however, with that British compassion. She felt herself responsible for the well-being of the human race, most of whom she believed to be under her jurisdiction.

"Mother, if you say 'oh' once more, I shall scream."

"What do your parents do, David?"

"My dad works in a factory and my mother . . ."

He didn't continue. Mother was beyond reach. She sulked behind her sherry glass and glanced, unblinking, from David to me. I could hear the tumblers in her mind.

Father, the dear, was easier. He took to David almost immediately. Unlike Mother, he could judge what a man could do rather than what he was. I only hoped Father wouldn't bring up the army. In his two years of service David had spent most of his time in the stockade, never rising above the rank of private. The nearest he'd ever gotten to high rank was, in fact, the sergeant major he'd punched in the mouth. David didn't particularly hate officers; he just hated the army. On one of our dates he had railed about the army; I told him quietly Father was a general. He blanched and then refused to take back what he'd said. I liked him for that.

David had given his word to behave with Father. What I hadn't realized was that they actually had something in common.

"Shelley tells me you make toys."

"Toys and games, sir. There's a huge market in them."

"Thank God. I'd hate another army man in the family. The silly bugger Andrew, my eldest y'know, joined. I tried to dissuade him. I hated it. How I became a general is a complete puzzle to me. Glad to meet someone with a business mind."

"It's still a small business."

"It'll grow. As a boy I had a most limited number of very stupid toys. Mostly damned breakable." Father stroked his moustache and studied David. "There are so many games one could play if someone was bright enough to make them."

"Well, if you have any ideas, sir, I'd be happy to work something out."

"You mean in the way of money?"

"Of course."

"Well, I do have a couple of things..."

Mother, perched on the edge of the chair, was glaring at the two of them.

"You're not going to marry him, are you?" she whispered as we went out for dinner.

"Yes. Isn't that what a properly brought up girl should do?"

"Rubbish." David was dismissed with a flick of her wrist. "You have absolutely nothing in common with..."

"David."

"... that man." She always used that phrase when she needed to irritate me. "You must marry someone from your own background. Anthony or Phillip or Auberon."

"How awful."

"What's wrong with them?"

"I think they'd fuck like good champagne gone flat."

She didn't flinch.

"David, I presume, is Guinness, or would it be stout. Bitter, crude and consumed in quantity."

"You should know I always made excessive demands as a child."

Shoulder to shoulder we swept into the dining room. The polished wooden floor gleamed in the soft light, the mahogany table was bright as a mirror. The table seated twelve. It was laid for four: lace table mats, gleaming silver and crystal and cool blue china. My brothers, one in the army and the other in the City, were unable to meet David that day. The room looked out through French doors onto the manicured lawn, orderly as a parade ground. Roses to the left, hyacinths to the right and not a leaf out of place. Fifty yards away, at the bottom, was a regiment of beeches. Darkness came early but the warmth lingered. We had the doors open.

Alton, Father's batman, served dinner. Mother and I sat side by side, David and Father opposite. The chairs at the head and foot of the table remained empty.

"Lust," Mother informed me, "should be practiced discreetly. Preferably out of the marriage bed."

David half cocked an ear, but Father was rambling and needed attention.

"And love?" I blew a kiss to David.

"Possibly that too."

"Is that your philosophy, Mother?" We looked at each other. Our eyes were alike, light green now and glittering.

"Occasionally." She leaned back to allow Alton to clear the dishes.

I looked at Father and David, both of them absorbed, then back to Mother. Her profile was sharp, unyielding. We sometimes, from only a word, catch glimpses of the people within our parents. Mother and lust? There had been opportunities. Like all army wives, lonely. Duty, work, the battlefront claim husbands yet somehow ignore lovers.

Where? Squirming, sweaty under a mosquito net in Delhi with a young subaltern? Or behind the Red Cross van with a plump, sleek Yank? I smiled.

"Don't stare, Shelley. It's bad manners." Motherhood reclaimed.

"What are you two whispering about?" Father asked.

"Girl talk, dear," waving Father back to David.

I had once asked, years back, why I was named Shelley. After a friend who read me the poetry, said Mother.

"I prefer both love and lust in the marriage bed," I said over Alton's arm as I helped myself to the pheasant.

"They wear out sooner than we think. Once they do, one needs compatibility."

"We have that already."

Momentarily, the poise left her, and I was allowed a quick glance deep into her heart. I saw the sadness.

"I hope so for your sake."

The poise returned to cover her eyes; she was resigned to David.

"I do so hate divorces in the family. They're pointless. People think the next one will be better. It never is, it's always the same."

Ooty Lane. I slowed and turned down it. The Empire lingered on; the names of strange towns carved on stone tablets ensured the traveler's memory of the past. There were a few gentle slopes to our left; empty pastured land sweeping down to meet the narrow lane. To the right lay undergrowth and, by the side of the road, a narrow pony trail. I had ridden it often. It led to a small open field where you could practice jumping. I seldom did, preferring the gallop over the fields.

The house was almost halfway down the lane. Creepers covered the east wing; the west was brown, rain-stained granite. I slowed and turned into the drive. The heavy oak door was open. The dogs came tumbling out, barking, nipping, wheeling. The children shouted, even Charles, and were playing to them before the car had stopped.

I left them and went in. Mother called from the study; she was sitting at her desk writing letters. Older, immaculately dressed, sunlight over her shoulder, she looked as perfectly delicate as a rose petal pressed between the silky pages of a nineteenth-century volume of poems. We kissed. Lilac powder, familiar as my pram.

"Father's upstairs. Writing memoirs."

"Still."

"Having reached Singapore, he's striking out to Mandalay." She listened to the children and the dogs, tilted her head to study me.

"David left me."

"Divorce?"

"No, I'm going to get him back. He's somewhere in America. I want to leave the children here."

"I'll get their rooms ready." Mother rose and would have sailed out to the linen cupboard.

"Aren't you going to say anything?"

She stood a foot away, gracefully awkward in midstride. The veins in her neck were light blue, the skin wrinkled. Having touched her neck countless times, my memory was of tight skin, forever smooth. I wanted to tear the layer of skin, this makeup of old age, from her neck. It wasn't really her face I saw but mine, of course. I tensed when I saw her about to speak. It was going to be an "I told you so." Instead, she touched my cheek with dry, soft fingers.

"Poor baby."

I wept. She held me. I sniffed and surfaced and wished she hadn't spoken, reducing me from a woman to an infant.

"I left your father once. And here I am still."

I feigned surprise. Three years ago, Father had told David about Mother's adventure. It *had* been a subaltern in fact, not in Delhi but in wet, cold Wales. Father had given her a couple of days with the man and then gone and fetched her back. I was born eleven months later. Father never did tell David what exactly had happened in the Welsh hills, what words he'd spoken, what he did to the man. In some ways I think they'd both forgotten most of it. We believe that passion illuminates our lives like a holocaust which will ravage us forever: then the sad day comes when we can no longer recall the insanity.

"Was it the man who read you Shelley?"

"Oh, no, dear." She smiled and left.

That man, I knew, was too precious to be given to me or any other person.

I spent the night, borrowed money for my American journey, and left the next day. Father had obviously been told. Just before dinner he patted my head, the way he used to when I was a child.

"What did he say when you told him?" I wanted to know.

Mother and the children and the dogs were walking me to the car. Father had returned to mopping up Mandalay.

"Nothing at first. Then he said if you're anything like him, you'll get David back." Then more to herself, "I believe he remembered."

"And you, Mother?"

"You know I haven't changed my mind about . . . that man. But you are—were—happy. And you taught him a lot."

"He did it to me as well."

She shrugged, very gently.

"Do you have to go there?"

"There" to Mother, a place she'd visited perhaps three times during our marriage, was David's parents.

"Yes. He may have told them something." I slid into the driving seat after kissing the children and Mother.

"Well, I suppose, give them my best."

"I shall, Mother. And I'll tell them you've invited them over for the weekend."

The children waved and then, like all children, ran back to play. Charles, my man, had already gone back into the house.

"Don't you dare." She held my hand on the steering wheel and added, "Good luck, Shelley."

Mother only unbent for the Warwicks at christenings. It wasn't quite all her fault; they were twitteringly nervous when she appeared on their horizons.

It had begun sunny, but an hour later as I headed east, bypassing London and snarling my way through ugly suburbs, the sky had begun to spit. The clouds were biblical; haloed by sunlight, dark in their centers.

Chelmsford was seventy miles the other side of London, and by the time I reached Baddow Road I was irritable, tired and quite hungry. I parked and sat. The semi-detached houses, prim, quiet, neat, ran along either side of the curving road like picket fences. They came in two colors: white and off-white.

We had sat in the old MG on a different grimy street. Four in the afternoon, a sunny day, and we were expected for tea. My hair was still in place under the silk scarf, but the heat of that old engine had made me perspire. I dabbed at my face, leaving spots in my makeup.

"You're okay, luv." David moved to get out.

"I'm not."

I was nervous. In other circumstances silence and shyness would have served to protect my dignity, but I wanted to be liked.

David grinned. He leaned across, a hand falling carelessly to my knee and sliding up past the top of my stocking to the flesh.

"You're beautiful."

"So are you."

I removed his hand from under my skirt, by chance looking up at the house. A curtain fell across a face. David didn't turn but caught the movement of my eyes.

"Mum, most probably." He got out of the car. "If she saw what I was doing she will no doubt disapprove of you. No nice girl allows a bloke to shove his hand up her skirt."

"Who said I was nice?" as we opened the small gate and crossed the crazy flagstones to the door. The steps were polished, the knocker smelt of Brasso.

"You're not respectable, either. All you've got is class, luv."

They were waiting; the door opened before I could answer. His mother was plump, friendly, nervous. The hallway was gloomy, cool and smelt of wax. By the time we reached the front room she'd informed me that David had told her everything about me.

"Everything?" I looked at David.

"Absolutely everything," he said as we entered the room.

It was a staged afternoon. Two flower-patterned overstuffed sofas faced each other, opposite the fireplace. There were pots without plants and half a dozen framed photographs. David, young, belligerent and stocky on a pier somewhere. The wind had blown his hair, his shirt was out. I touched the picture.

We sat down, two to a sofa. His father was surprisingly small. He wore a dark suit as if it were armor, the tie an arrow sticking in his throat. He sat quietly, letting his wife talk, sometimes smiling. I could see where David got his smile.

"Your father doesn't say much," I said when they left to fetch the tea.

"I told him to shut up."

"Why, for heaven's sake?"

"I'll tell you later."

"Now."

"He's a socialist, voted for the Labour Party all his life, and when I told him about you the first question he asked—after a long silence, mind you—what party does she vote for? I guessed Tory, and he choked on his fucking beer. He hates Tories, thinks they're all fairies and parasites. Most probably you're the first one he's ever met. Anyway, I told him if he started on politics, I'd shove my fist down his throat."

"Bully."

"Twenty-five years I've known that man. He's small but he's a bloody-minded little scrapper. If you can stand up to him, you can take on the world."

Over the years we got to be friends. We never talked politics except in the most polite possible way. He'd turn red in the face to control himself in front of this Tory. A toolmaker, he took me once to the factory and showed me where he'd spent forty years of his life. It was gloomy and quiet and smelt of oil, a sad cage with sunlight filtering through the skylights. As he told me how his machine worked, I touched a seam of bitterness.

"You have to be careful," he said. "It cuts your hands sometimes and," he paused, staring at it, "more often your heart."

I felt I came from a light, airy world remote from him and that though we stood side by side, related, we were forever strangers. I took his hand, palm up. It was scarred and brutally calloused. David's hands were soft, the nails manicured.

The others had come in during tea, cued in and out by David. His brother Derek, slightly smaller than David, an apprentice in the factory. Derek's girl friend Mary, sweet. Then Hillary, the sister, with short dark hair and a smile. Each stayed minutes—there wasn't enough space to seat everyone—and then caught a signal from David and faded.

It was all very formal. David, and I was pleased, never apologized for anything.

He showed me his room, so small and cramped, overlooking the backyard. I looked around and found little of him in it.

"If we have a quick screw here I suppose they'll all hear." I reached out, he stepped back.

"Sometimes I think you have the makings of a whore."

"Be thankful for that, darling," I kissed him before he could move. "Two centuries of family decadence could have marked me in a more terrible way."

"And here I was thinking that was the worst," leading me out before he succumbed.

"You'll learn, angel. Class has always been a license for marvelous depravities."

I didn't use the front door—only strangers did. I walked carefully down the narrow concrete path, worn and chipped, that ran alongside the left side of the house. I hesitated, wanting to confront them separately rather than together. Otherwise it would be like facing a court of inquiry. She, blandly understanding, silently condemning me for our failure; he impartial but not committed, for it would create a schism between them.

I moved past the kitchen window; Mum stood at the sink. I waved and kept moving toward the tiny shack at the bottom of the yard. The size of a closet, but it was his refuge from the family.

A workbench, cluttered with tools and shavings, took up most of the space. There wasn't room for me as well, so I stood by the door. It had been eight months since we'd visited. He seemed smaller, supporting, by the stoop of his shoulders, the exhaustion of fifty years in a factory. Constant obedience to a machine had humbled him. Gray hair fringed a pink damp patch on his head; his eyes were framed by cheap steel-rimmed spectacles. Only his hands were still sure—they would never forget their trade. A soggy brown, thinly rolled cigarette stuck to his lips.

When we kissed, I smelt the familiar odors of oil and tobacco and perspiration. He only had to glance expectantly out of the small, curtained window.

I told him.

"I didn't even know, lass, till now." He lit the stub of the cigarette and shook his head. "We haven't heard from David, least not me, maybe Mary has. He came—oh, two months ago—for an hour." He rubbed the gray stubble on his chin. "I think he left a jacket here. Mary has it in the cupboard. Come and have some tea." He put an arm around my waist and hugged. "You were good for him, you know. At first I thought you were right stuck up, especially the way you spoke. Took me time to realize that you weren't putting it on. It was natural. You're my favorite, now."

We went out, entwined. He felt brittle against my hip.

There was tea, there were chocolate biscuits. Mary was flustered; she enjoyed tarting up the occasion, as I was unexpected. Yet beneath the flutterings she managed to sense the reason for my visit. Easy for her: I was alone.

"That's really surprising, really surprising." She looked at her husband. "Surprising, isn't it?" He nodded. "David never told me nothing. He never did anyway, always kept himself to himself. And you didn't know, did you, Shelley?"

"No." I was wanting to return to my house. I couldn't call it home. There would be no one there but me. "You're sure he didn't tell you anything?"

"He never did," she repeated. "Last time he came he only dropped in for a cup of tea. Forgot his jacket. Do you want it or . . ."

"I'll take it."

She hesitated. David hovered between us, a spirit who could not rightly be claimed by either. She had the stronger claim, for there is no divorce between mother and child.

"Give it to her."

She rose, somewhat grudgingly, and fetched it for me. It was the brown leather short coat I'd bought him, knowing how handsome he would look in it. There were creases in the leather, and the pockets sagged from the weight of his hands. It smelt of David and I held on to it, tightly, until I finished the tea and got into the car. His father walked me to it; Mary watched through the lace curtains.

"If you need anything, ask me. I haven't got much but . . ."

I kissed him again.

As I took the jacket out of the car, the envelope fell out of the inside pocket.

CHAPTER 4

A DOZEN TIMES ON THE FLIGHT I READ THE POSTCARD that had lived in the envelope. Her writing was neat and uniform, with tiny circles above the *i*'s. The lines sloped slightly downward.

> *My dearest, dearest D:*
>
> I just cannot believe that you are coming to me so soon. I can't believe that I can have such love again, or that it could have happened so suddenly. I miss you, my darling—if only you could be with me this very moment, I'd be so happy. This could be a dream—you don't really exist. I will only stop being afraid when I touch you. Ring me at (212) 622-8514 the moment you book your flight. I'll be waiting.
>
> *Love, lots, C.*

I turned it over. On the other side there was a lovely photograph of Rodin's "Lovers."

I had forgotten America. The week spent with David five years ago had faded, leaving only fragments of distaste for New York. I hadn't liked the noise and the size and the hurry.

I shrank back into the seat of the yellow cab, remembering the harsh accent of the driver, trying to recognize the bills—all the same size—and translating to pounds as I counted, surreptitiously. The lights were on everywhere, as if the people were afraid of the dark; the sizes of things ranged from large to enormous. Nations live to the scale of their landscape: England, in comparison, was minute and dainty.

As the taxi climbed to the bridge, I recalled one pleasure. Across the river in the fading summer light was the skyline, a silhouetted stage set. I stared, then sank back. I had visited only once and yet there was nothing unfamiliar, nothing strange, nothing to be discovered.

The Plaza, because we'd stayed there, was the only hotel I could think of. I had liked the European granite facade, the green roof, the Palm Court with orchestra, a sort of Viennese Grosvenor.

"Mrs. Warwick. I booked a room."

She checked. I took the card and began to fill it in.

"Shelley!"

My pen skidded. The voice—English, male—was teasingly familiar. I wrote steadily.

"Shelley!"

Softer, closer; still no face or name. Yet obviously the bastard knew me. I returned the card and turned, my face prepared for a suitably hostile expression.

"Oh, my god!"

My eyes closed for a moment. When they opened, he hadn't disappeared. He reached out to take my limp hand and hold it.

"I believe that's mine." I withdrew my hand and followed the bellboy. "How are you, Chapman?"

How long? Three years, four years? A weekend in Monte Carlo, buried in the avalanche of days and years. He should have remained buried, instead of resurrecting. And following me. And tipping the bellboy to take my cases to the room.

"I do *not* want a drink in the Oak Bar, Chapman." The bellboy had detached himself; I hurried. "I'm tired."

"It'll pick you up, Shelley."

"I prefer remaining fallen, crumpled, or whatever's the opposite to being 'picked up.' " He smiled; another David. Save me from a world of strong men. "Stop playing the grande dame, Shelley." He was edging me away from the elevator in the direction of the bar. "You know a drink will make you feel better."

I took off the dark glasses. His hair was grayer and curled over the nape of his neck; the half-cheeked sideburns were distinguished; the moustache, clipped and rakish. He looked, in fact, like Errol Flynn.

"How on earth did you remember me?"

"Out of the millions?" When he smiled it was cheeky. "You shouldn't screw so well."

Loud enough for the bellboy and two ladies to swivel their heads. The elevator doors opened and they stepped in and turned expectantly.

"I'll have that drink, only one."

"Knew you would." He took my arm; I untook it. "I lost that damned race, you know, because of you. Lapse of concentration when I had the blasted thing in my pocket. I needed it for the championship."

"I thought you deliberately drove into the bale of hay."

I had watched the race with David the next day, full of passion for my husband not out of guilt but out of waiting; tingling, douched and ready for another run.

Chapman had been needed only as a sexual interlude, not as a lover—long or short term.

He winced. "Misjudged that corner, took it too fast."

The Oak Bar was crowded, but Chapman was seated immediately by a window looking out on Central Park.

"I tried to reach you after the race."

"My husband." I felt that was enough.

"Is he here now? You checked in alone."

"He's in America."

"I'm staying in the hotel as well." He smiled.

"How nice for you."

That smile had me stripped, splayed, and no doubt expectant on his double bed, or mine, with champagne on the side table and some awful background music dribbling into my ear. I wasn't feeling Pavlovian as I ordered my drink.

I glanced around the room. The humming elegance was as I remembered it. As were the scrupulously clean men in their three-piece suits, and the almost too perfectly lovely women.

"That was a great weekend, Shelley."

By stirring memory, he hoped to stir passion.

"Was it?"

David and I had sat together, also by a window here, three or four tables down. David had a business dinner, and I had come down alone, feeling selfish and hurtful, to sulk and guzzle vodkas. I wasn't happy. Three days in New York, free from children, alone with David, and the city pinched my nerve ends. The sirens never stopped, the drizzle was constant, I was never alone with David, and as a preconditioned European I had decided not to like the city. It was lying, gritty and rough, somewhere below the outer layer of my skin, right against the soft tissues.

David loved New York. Here, released from background and upbringing, identifiable only as an Englishman, he spiraled and waltzed, a free spirit. On my second drink, he came and slid into the vacant seat.

"What's the matter, luv?" As if he didn't know.

"Don't call me 'luv.'"

"You didn't mind it before."

"I didn't mind diapers either."

"Shit."

We sat, separated by a table and thirteen years of knowledge of each other. Lovers, friends, acquaintances, husband and wife, partners, we maintained our silence and stared out at the shining street, shielding our knowledge from ourselves and each other. Two strangers, meeting in a singles bar, could not have been more distant.

"Okay," he said finally. "You don't like New York."

"I don't mind New York that much. It's you. Running around like the original Horatio Alger."

"Who's he? Don't bother. He's a working-class lad who made it. He have an upper-class wife?"

"I never finished the book." I didn't like the undercurrents in his voice. He didn't back down; only reined in.

"I'm sorry, Shelley." His hands, so large and gentle, gestured knowledgeably. "I've always liked New York. They give you chances, you can make money here. You know . . . it's adrenalin."

"Or fumes going to your head." My turn now. "I feel like a pilot fish, detached from you and swimming around. Saks, Bloomingdale's, Gucci."

"Pilot fish swim in front."

"Well, I'm a back-swimming pilot fish, following and not knowing where the hell I'm going."

"This isn't Cannes or Florence or Beirut for me, Shelley. I'm working. I just wanted to have you with me. You'd never been to New York and . . ."

"I know." I stroked his head absentmindedly. "Do

you have to always work so hard? Meetings, dinners, meetings. What more do we need, darling?"

"I told you at the beginning that I would become a millionaire." He dropped his years; his face slimmed and his eyes brightened as he remembered his own arrogance.

"How far away are you?"

"It's not a matter of how far. I can be even better than I dreamed. I've got the chance. F. A. O. Schwarz are going to give me a huge contract. That's the breakthrough I needed."

"So you become a multimillionaire, then a billionaire. Then what?" Maybe I sneered, I don't remember. He moved off onto a tangent.

"You've had money all your life. You don't even understand what I mean or where I came from."

"I do." He was looking dangerous. "I married you when you were poor and we lived in Finchley. Besides, your parents aren't exactly from the ghetto." Father had offered to lend us some money then, but I'd refused. If David had found out, there would have been a godalmighty row.

"Finchley, for Christ's sake. If that's poverty to you . . ."

"It was, and bloody lonely."

Finchley! I didn't even know such a place existed. I knew no one there; my friends were in Belgravia and Knightsbridge and South Kensington and a dozen different places. Everywhere except Finchley. A wasteland of supermarkets and pubs, dry cleaners and cold flats.

"Well, now you're in Hampstead." He hesitated, then it rushed out. "If we moved to New York, I could have you living on . . . Fifth Avenue."

"Which end?"

"The best one." He said it quietly, but I knew he was itching to slap me or spank me.

Only once had he slapped me. It was in the first year

of our marriage. The incident that caused it must have been minor for I can't remember it. I was so surprised that I reacted with a punch to his jaw that actually floored him. He swore he'd lost his balance.

"And what about the children, David? Do they have any schools in New York or only cages?"

I had countless objections and, given time, I could have thought up a few more. I was reacting as fast as I could; it was the first I'd known that he was actually considering a move. We would have battled on but were saved by our guests. We both smiled at them like lovers and ignored each other for the rest of the evening.

Chapman charmed, made jokes, flirted. The stops were all out. Virtually wasted, as I wasn't paying attention. I was crumbling from a month's exhaustion inside: the cells were falling like scattered toys, my brain was trying to slip down my spine. David was near and so was Miss C. Schraft, and I needed to be ready.

"You're wasting a good line of chat, Chapman. I'm going to bed. Alone."

"Nothing's ever wasted."

I finished my drink and wished I hadn't been so inventive that weekend. He wasn't going to give up easily.

"There are beautiful girls in New York, Chapman."

"All nuts."

"And aren't you athletes supposed to rest before the big race?" I stood up and prepared to sweep out of the room. "Remember what happened last time?"

"Didn't you know I retired?" The little dent in his ego seemed to make his moustache uncurl.

"I don't read the sports pages."

"I made the front pages."

"Those either."

I did vaguely recall his retirement, but it never hurt to throw a little cold water.

He stood up and kissed my hand lightly. "I'm going to be here a few days. I'm sure you'll be able to have dinner another day, when your husband's too busy."

"With your wife, I hope?"

"We've separated." Now his face brightened, as if he'd just had an idea. It had, I was sure, been simmering for the last half hour. "Maybe you'd like to spend a weekend in Watkins Glen with me. I have to plug a motor oil."

"I'd hate to make that a threesome. Good-night, Chapman."

He hesitated, hovered and dropped back into his seat. He wasn't going to give up all hope for that evening. I was on ice for a few days; there were others to be pursued.

My room, pretty and comfortable, was on the twelfth floor, overlooking the park.

It had been many years since I had stayed alone in a hotel room. It seemed as if I had aged, yet time hadn't changed. It held me still and barren: children, husband, home—all seemed to have slipped through my body. Even Chapman would have been better than this.

The park, a pit in a field of lights, stretched out as far as I could see. The carriages were still lining the street, the horses patient, the men standing in twos and threes. The traffic was endless and those bloody sirens sounded again in the distance.

I took the coin case and her postcard out of my purse.

I needed to keep moving. I dialed her number, not knowing who would answer or what I would say. It rang and rang; finally I replaced the receiver and prepared for bed.

When I awoke, late, the park looked beautiful. It was the surroundings that were drab. Part of the pleasure of overlooking open space was that I could stand nude at the window, letting the sun brush and brighten my body. I was glad for the weather; this day was going to be an important one for me.

It had been over two months since I had practiced yoga. For over a year it had been part of a daily ritual: I had used it the same way I used dressing the girls, making breakfast, kissing David good-bye each morning, bathing and carefully dressing. It was a way of piecing myself together, like a knight donning armor and readying for the day's battle. I retreated now to that ritual.

Two hours later, I was as composed as I would ever be. I dialed the number. If she answered . . . I wouldn't think. It rang only once.

"Ingersol's, good-morning."

Oh dear, what the hell was that?

"May I speak to Miss Schraft, please?" I waited, not breathing, not being alive for a few moments.

"I'm afraid she's no longer with the firm. Can someone else be of help to you? I can connect you to Miss Martin."

"No, thank you . . . Could you tell me what your firm does?"

"We're interior decorators."

"Would you know where I could reach Miss Schraft?" I hesitated. "She's a personal friend, you see."

"Miss Martin may be of help."

"She's started her own firm," said Miss Martin, who sounded vaguely southern to my ignorant ear. "It's on Third Avenue and she calls it Schraft's . . ." She laughed at the originality of the name. "I have the number somewhere."

I took it down. "Then she's also an interior decorator?"

"Yes. In fact she had my position, then she managed to start her own shop a couple of months back."

"Thank you very much."

I smoked and sat and paced the floor and stared out

of the window thinking how to meet Miss Schraft. I would not tell her I was the abandoned woman, I could not claim remote acquaintance, I could not be a friend of a friend. I had to be a stranger to her, befriend her and then . . .

By twelve o'clock I was ready to move. I lunched lightly, a salad, and then walked along Central Park South. Passing the sign on a towering apartment block at the corner of Seventh, I stopped and looked up at it. The glass and steel were hardly to my taste—I would have preferred something older and less expensive—yet it was impressive enough.

The view from the thirtieth floor was magnificent. North I looked out over the park, south I looked straight down Seventh Avenue. I took a two-bedroom apartment on a six-month lease.

I hummed, walking back to the hotel three hours later. The day was glorious and that clear blue sky seemed to have slipped inside me. I felt like a child aching to boast of her cleverness. There was no one, but that couldn't damage the feeling. When I reached the hotel there was a message from Chapman: he wanted to wine and dine me that evening. I left a message in his pigeonhole: Yes.

The receptionist gave me directions to Louis Guy d' and fixed an appointment for me. I decided that walking around a few blocks would give me time to think how I should wear my hair. Glancing into a window, I had recognized myself too easily. I'd looked the same for the last ten years—same style, same length, same color—and no doubt David had a few snapshots of me. He might have shown the victim to Miss Schraft; it was a chance I didn't want to take.

I strolled along, scrutinizing other women's hair styles. Louis Guy d' was above street level. Having made up my mind while walking, I nonetheless took the chair with no certainty whatsoever. I was to look as different as possible, and I had liked my familiar self.

Two and a half hours later, having glared in the mirror at the casual performance of each step, I was finished.

"Blond hair suits you a *lot* better," said the stylist. "And so does the new length. You'll have to touch up the roots every few weeks, of course."

"Of course." I hated it.

I hurried back to the Plaza. Wanting to hide, I made straight for the bathroom mirror.

My reflection stared back at me. Pageboyish, longer at the back, and a sullen face framed in honey-colored hair. The eyebrows were plucked, narrow spears. I could even have had a bloody nose job. It was certainly different.

"What a fuck-up I've made."

I brushed it furiously in half a dozen different ways. It fell back to its setting.

The phone rang. It was Chapman.

"I'm downstairs. Want me to come up?"

"Stay there. Have a drink or something. I'll be down in fifteen minutes."

"We could have dinner in your room."

"It's too intimate for my taste, Chapman." I dropped the phone. It was going to be one of those evenings: fencing off Scaramouche with my back to a cliff.

I wore a suit, inappropriate for dinner, but simple and severe enough to keep Charpman's intentions to a minimum. Half a revealed breast and he would think we were back in Monte Carlo.

"Don't you like it?" as I slid into my seat at the bar.

Chapman tilted his head and studied me. I smiled defensively and ordered a vodka. It would be my only drink for the evening.

"You look smashing. Why'd you do it?"

"I just wanted a change."

"Change is bloody right." He examined my hair. "And it's not a wig!"

68

"No. Where are you taking me to dinner?"

"A place in the Village. Does your husband approve? I mean your hair, not me."

"He would disapprove of both."

Chapman smiled, patted my hand, and let it rest once he'd touched. I wriggled it out from under.

"Kicking up your heels in a big city, are you?"

"Not in the way you think, Chapman." I finished my drink and felt better. The difference in hair was enough to make Chapman look twice. A stranger, acquainted only with a snapshot, would have to study me closer.

At dinner I drank Perrier, to Chapman's disgust. The restaurant, pretty and crowded, was called One If By Land, Two If By Sea. Over the first course he asked me the question I was hoping he'd forgotten.

"Where is your husband, Shelley?"

"Visiting Topeka. That's in Kansas, I think."

"So I heard."

It was said in a tone of suspended disbelief, but he didn't add to it and I felt he was waiting to pounce with some wisp of knowledge tucked away in the back of his mind.

"Why did you separate, Chapman?" over the Beef Wellington, a new invention to me and very well prepared.

"She fell in love with someone else."

"And you let her go?"

He paused in mid-chew, then said softly, "Yes."

"After how many years?"

"Twenty. I met her when I was a garage mechanic trying to get a few drives in Saloon cars around Brand's Hatch." He answered before I asked: "Only two children, and they're both in college. I suppose we could have gone for another twenty years."

"Why didn't you then?"

"She wanted out."

"Did she really? You know that for sure?"

"We both made the decision. She wanted to go, I let

her. Twenty years!" He shook his head, as if disbelieving the tricks time played on people. "She took a lot, you know. I admired her, she'd come and watch me drive and keep time. I would see her face. The skin was tight as a bloody drum. It doesn't bother us, we're busy driving, thinking, calculating. But it's cruel to them. Especially when they see another driver die and they have to comfort the poor bloody widow."

"Is that why you retired?"

"Yes." He stared into the distance. "Well, partly. I was also not winning."

It was as important to him as an erection; the destruction must have begun then, eroding the affection. She hadn't for all those years been afraid of his death; he and she had lived with that. It was his failure that neither of them could live with. Suddenly he seemed faded and frayed. He did not want the new conquest, the terror of exploration. He wanted to recapture the old; to remember the Monte Carlo days when he won, and often.

"He's left you, hasn't he?"

"Who?"

"Whatever his name is, Dick, Fred, Peter. Your husband, luv."

"David. And don't call me 'luv' . . . How do you know?"

"I'm looking into a mirror, and I see myself."

"You'd look pretty in a dark blond pageboy." The joke didn't raise a smile. "It's only temporary," I added. "I want another eighteen years with him."

"Does he?"

I pressed my knuckles to my face, indenting so hard that my cheek hurt.

"Don't ask me questions I can't answer, Chapman. The world is so full of them. Ask me one I can. I'm here to get him back."

"Lucky man." He folded his napkin and signaled for the check. "Let's get back to the hotel."

We waited until the waiter returned his credit card. The question hung between us as we threaded our way through the crowd to the exit. We were lucky; a taxi was just pulling up to empty passengers. Its scratched plastic partition hid the driver from view and hearing. "Not tonight, Chapman," I said as the cab began the long run up Sixth Avenue. "I tried it with someone else not long ago, and it didn't work."

He patted my hand and didn't try to hold on. We were both very alone, and so distant from each other.

"What's she like? The bird he went with, I mean."

"I don't know. I'm going to meet her tomorrow. I'll tell you then."

CHAPTER 5

"Good-morning, Schraft's."

"May I speak to Miss Schraft."

"This is Miss Schraft speaking."

Her voice grated: it was pleasant, cheerful and enthusiastic. This was going to be difficult. With my eyes and mouth, I had to like her enough to become her friend. The violence must lie hidden beneath. I'd have to keep the two feelings apart, not letting one wash into the other—warning her on the one hand, diluting me on the other. If only her voice had been dreadfully, nasally American.

"Can I help you?"

The pause widened in front of me. All my preparations, even down to the written notes in front of me on the table, were forgotten. I was fighting not for breath but for calmness.

"Yes." The burst was too loud, I toned it down. "Yes, you can. I've just moved to New York, and I've got this super apartment on Central Park South. I heard about you from some friends in Los Angeles and . . ."

"Who?"

"The Morrises. I don't think you met them but they saw something you'd decorated and admired your work very much, Miss Schraft."

"Call me Candice . . ."

That helped. An awful name, nowhere near as good as Cunt. It sounded so artificial to my ear. Canned ice. Candy. Marvelously appropriate; sweet, sugary, and indigestible.

"What a lovely name!" I retreated from the treacle. That could come later. "To cut a long story short, Candice, I'd love you to have a look at this apartment, and maybe, if you're not too busy, do the decorating."

"Well, I am rather busy, but I'd certainly like to have a look at it, Mrs. . . . ?"

"Patricia." A name I always wished I'd been given. Samantha was also a favorite; Miranda had been David's choice, no doubt after a duchess seen in *Harper's Bazaar*. "Patricia Middleton, and it's . . . Miss."

To hell with it. I had been Mrs. for eighteen years and with the change in name and face I might as well have the fun of changing my marital status.

"Excuse me, Patricia."

She had turned away from the phone.

Was David there with her? I closed my eyes tight. If he was listening in on an extension, my voice was as familiar to him as his was to me. I strained to hear: she was only turning pages.

"I have a morning free at the end of the week . . ."

"Oh, couldn't you do it earlier, please? It's just that I'm staying in a hotel and I'd love to move in as soon as possible."

"Well . . ." she teetered and fell, "maybe tomorrow morning. I'll have to study the project before I could possibly commit myself, of course. Shall we meet in your hotel?"

"Oh, let's meet at the apartment." I gave her the address.

"You're English, aren't you?"

Now that was quite clever.

"Yes, I am. How did you guess?"

"I spent a few months in England, earlier this year" (as if I didn't know that, you stupid cow) "and I really love your country."

"I'm glad." I bit my tongue to stop, but it came out: "Did you pick up any . . . souvenirs?"

"Oh, yes, I shopped nonstop. Harrods, Marks, Selfridges . . ." And Kutchinsky's, my dear.

She would have gone on, but I knew that if she did I would make a very bitchy remark. All my years as a very proper lady, and I discover at this late date that I have more bitch in me than a dozen alley cats.

"You must tell me everything, and I mean that literally, tomorrow. I have to fly now, Candice. Bye."

It was over. I sat, shaking and peculiarly exhausted. It felt as if I had been near death and this was the aftermath of the confrontation. It was only eleven, but I drank two fingers of vodka straight. It hit my stomach with the impact of a brick. I coughed and sat down very slowly. It quieted me; my stomach unwound and my head cleared.

I had, in terms that would show up in Father's memoirs, probed and made contact with the enemy. I wasn't too happy following Father's military tactics; like most generals, he lost more men than he gained ground—more often than not the wrong piece of earth. I really didn't want to fight a rearguard action, whatever that meant militarily: it sounded too much like a defeat. What came next? Air cover?

I phoned home for advice. I knew what needed to be done and yet, feeling like a child, I wanted comforting and reassurance. Mother came on the line.

"David phoned for you. He sounded rather frantic."

"Good. What did you say?"

"Oh, the truth."

"Mother!"

"That you were out hunting. Any luck?"

"Some. How are the children?"

"They miss you but otherwise they're fine."

"Give them my love. Can I speak to Dad?"

"What on earth for?"

"Just get him, Mother."

It took him a long minute, and I imagined he'd lost his way from the study to the hall. How he found Singapore was beyond me.

"Daddy, it's me. Silly." It had been his nickname for me ever since I mispronounced my own name as a small child. I used it when I needed to be the child again. "I need your help. I'm here now. What should I do?"

"Have you met David?"

"Do you think I should?"

"No." I listened patiently to the humming wires. He'd think of something for me. He'd never let me down as yet. "I would suspect that the first step would be to find out how the land lies. If you make contact with the enemy too early you could suffer heavy losses and it would take a long time to regroup. Surprise is going to be your strongest weapon. What do you know about the enemy?"

"Her name is Candice Schraft."

"That's not enough, Silly. Since you can't send out a reconnoitering party, you'll have to do the work yourself."

"What should I find out, Daddy?"

"Everything possible. Her weaknesses, her strengths. What her strike capabilities are, and how she moves in defense. You've got to ask her friends, her enemies, anyone you can get to who knows her. So that when you do make contact, you're well prepared to do battle."

"That's going to be the difficult part, you know."

"I know. Weighing up your situation, I'd advise a lightning strike the moment you find the weakness. Don't try to fight a long battle, Silly. Your logistics lines are too extended, you're on her territory, and you could lose the hostage. And Silly . . ."

"Yes, Daddy?"

"Good luck."

Intelligence! I had to know more about Candice. How easily her name tripped off my tongue. If I could only hire the CIA, I would have them dig up all the dirt. Even to the days her period started and stopped.

"Miss Martin, please." She was my original informer and underlings are usually brimming with gossip, hopefully the worst. "This is Miss Middleton, Patricia Middleton. I spoke to you yesterday . . ."

"I recognize your voice. You were asking about Miss Schraft."

"That's right, Miss Martin."

"Rikki . . ." Americans drop their first names the way salesmen leave calling cards. An easy way to informality and the quick parting.

"Rikki—and do call me Patricia—I've just leased an apartment and I wondered whether I could consult you about having it decorated."

"I'm very busy, Patricia, but I may be able to make it next week. Where is it?"

"Central Park South. Two bedrooms on the thirtieth floor." I sensed her reaction to the address. "If I may come across for half an hour and just tell you what I'm interested in, you could inspect it next week."

"I've got half an hour free at twelve-thirty."

"That'll be fine."

I rang off quickly. My preoccupations were gone. I sensed and saw bright and clearly. Stepping out of the Plaza, I noticed the sudden rush of warmth. The city streets wavered in front of me as I climbed into the old smelly taxi. The seat was sticky and I sat on its edge like an Alsatian with his nose held high. It didn't help.

The heat in New York seemed far worse than it had

during the three-week safari in Kenya with David. The oppressiveness there had been partly relieved by the space and, because I had been with him, I hadn't felt the same depression. Ever since the childhood spent in that dismal town of his birth, he had yearned to go on a safari. It was his dream, not so much of leisure as of luxury. There were times when I loved him more than at other times. In Kenya I had flowed and ached with love until the pain was almost unbearable. David, in some ways, never changed; he had retained both his innocence and his energy all through our life together. I, the sophisticate, the cultured, the civilized—if not the world weary at least the déjà vuer—had only a partial effect on him. He learned what I could teach him the way a child does, eagerly, but it didn't stifle him.

In Kenya he had explored the country and the people and the animals with the passion of a boy. He had charmed the Kikuyu off his one-legged perch, cajoled the white settlers into lowering their reserve for this working-class man they would have held at a distance in their mother country, and he stalked the animals with all his cameras. At night, he had loved me as if we'd just met in that rubble-strewn dirty house.

The ride through those few blocks took fifteen minutes. Entering the building was like slipping through a current of cool water in a warm river.

Rikki Martin was a small, dark-haired woman in her early twenties. She was pretty in a foxy way; quick gray eyes and an easy mouth, a bit too full for her face. She sat in a small, cluttered office that displayed a dazzle of swatches, a couple of Mexican masks, pewter mugs, a copper engraving. Too much to be seen in a glance. Miss Martin—not "Rikki" to me—was leaning forward, head at a tilt, the smile ready.

I described what I wanted in this fantasy apartment suspended high above a park in a strange city. I might have paid out some money and signed the lease, but it would always remain unreal.

"It sounds as if it's something we could be interested in, Patricia."

"Well, think about it. When we meet next week you can get down to work. I was going to contact Miss Schraft but then I thought perhaps I should consult an established firm like yours."

"Oh, I'm so glad you did," she hesitated. "Do you know Candice well?"

"We've never met."

A quick look of satisfaction came across her face and she nodded, just a shade too wisely. I was convinced that I had detected an enemy of Candice's, one who could surely be useful.

"Candice is a very talented person. Very." She bent to light her cigarette. "But she's also erratic. If you know what I mean?"

"I'm afraid I don't." And then I decided to commit myself. "I'm trying to find out a few things about Candice . . . for personal reasons."

Rikki stopped mid-puff and after a moment let the smoke out languidly.

"Personal?" She closed her eyes and the lashes threw vertical crow marks. "Such as?"

I intended to use her, but not as a confessional.

"What do you mean by erratic?"

She shrugged. The curiosity was still there but for the moment, I thought, she'd decided to lay it aside.

"Up. Down. She's like a goddamned elevator. One day she's turning in great work. The next . . . pure shit. Guess who had to keep covering for her?"

"Why did she leave your firm?"

"She didn't quite . . . leave. But I can't say she was fired either. Let's say, she beat Jack to the punch." She noticed my raised eyebrow. "Jack's the owner. They never got along well together."

"Whose fault do you think it was? Candice's?"

"You bet. Jack's a real sweet man."

Possibly a love affair? Her defense seemed a bit strong for Jack.

"Why was he going to fire her?"

"She has very expensive tastes... which isn't a bad habit in this business, but she wouldn't compromise, either. And, she always thought she knew more than Jack." She leaned over to stub out her cigarette and I caught the sly glint in her eye. "And, of course, the problems with customers."

"How do you mean?"

"She used to get involved with them. I mean... the men. You should have a small talk with John Richmond. She did his apartment. I know she had an affair with him. I figured she was trying to get him to bankroll her. I guess she found another sucker."

I flushed and nearly committed myself to my dear sucker's defense. The moment passed, and icy calm returned.

"I gather you didn't get on well with her at all."

"You kidding? She was... just too emotional. One day she's all hearts and flowers and the next day she lets us all enjoy the benefit of her temper. How the hell can you work with someone like that?"

I stood and extended my hand so our fingertips just touched. I'd decided not to discard her immediately—I might need her again.

"Do you have John Richmond's number?"

She flicked through her phone book and wrote it down on her pad. She didn't hand it over immediately but dangled it an inch away.

"You won't mention our meeting, will you?"

"I shan't, if you won't."

I took the paper and she came round to walk me to the door.

"Rikki, do you think you could find out something about her new business?"

"Of course, Patricia. And do keep in touch. I'd love to hear what happens."

I rang John Richmond from a telephone booth in the lobby.

"Mr. Richmond?" as breathy as possible.

"Yes."

"My name's Susan Hudson. We haven't met before but I've heard what a marvelous job your decorator did on your apartment—Candice Schraft is her name, isn't it?—and I'd love to see for myself."

"Well . . ."

"I'm thinking about commissioning Miss Schraft to do mine, and if I could just get an idea . . ."

"I'd be delighted." He sounded slick. "I'm on Riverside Drive. Why don't you come now?"

Richmond, in his midforties, was rich and too polished. All glitter, with the decay well camouflaged under the open-neck silk shirt, tailored slacks, and rub-on sun tan. As a lover he would perspire and slide. How she could have my David after him was incomprehensible.

"Thank you so much, Mr. Richmond. I'm a fan of Candice's kind of work and I really might want her to do my place."

He stepped aside, looking me up and down. At times, eyes can be stubby fingers.

"Any fan of hers is welcome."

The sitting room, facing the shimmering river, was done in my favorite colors: beiges and browns. I liked it. Damn! I had been hoping, imagining, that Canned Ice would have gone for plastic, neon, steel and whorehouse red. She had spent Richmond's money well. The Chinese lacquer screen was lovely and suited the teak cabinet; the settees contrasted nicely with the oat-colored carpet. It was frighteningly close to what I would have done.

"She really is talented."

"I guess so."

His enthusiasm for her waned as his eyes dropped a fraction to my breasts.

"Would you like to see the rest, Miss . . ." He glanced at my ringless fingers. ". . . Hudson?"

"Thank you."

The dining room: gleaming mahogany and velvet-backed chairs. I touched the sideboard, wanting it briefly. The kitchen was an array of gadgets. Richmond crossed quickly to a door and entered it, leaving it open. Sensing the bedroom, I stood poised on the threshold. Candice liked using woods the way I did. The dresser and the bed were dark and warm; the mirror above the bed was the only thing I didn't like. I stepped back into the hall. He followed me back to the sitting room, leaving the bedroom door open.

"A drink?"

"Thank you, vodka."

He poured while I wandered. I stopped and turned.

"What's Candice like?"

It was, possibly, too abrupt.

"She's very clever. Sharp as a razor and quite funny. She knows how to make you laugh. I mean me."

That would take only a clown's costume for him. I took the drink, sat in a chair. He took the sofa.

"And she is—was—very inventive." He was smiling.

How simple men are. Tickle their armpits and they think you've discovered a new method of ejaculation for them.

"Did you know her for a long time?"

"We were close friends for a month. I couldn't have taken it longer than that."

He looked as if with a bit of coaxing he'd be happy to be even more indiscreet.

"Taken it? But I gather she's a lovely girl."

"She is, but she does have some peculiar habits. She used to adopt things. Cats, dogs, people, even cockroaches. Her apartment in the West Village was like the crossroads of two jungle trails. She got me involved with all her animals and people."

"That sounds funny."

"It isn't when you're involved. I think that was her ecological phase. She must be onto something else now."

"Probably she is." I crossed the room and I looked out of the window. Certainly a romantic view. "Is she temperamental?"

"Very. When she's happy she's a marvelous person to be with. It's really being alive." His voice became surprisingly gentle as he remembered. "But her downs are deep."

"Does she get drunk when she's down?" I wandered back and sat a bit farther away.

"No. Just very moody and kind of menacing. In a ... self-destructive way. It's a total loss of confidence, really." He shrugged. "I just couldn't take what she'd hand out during those spells."

Including temper, I imagined, remembering Rikki's comments. "Some women have affairs when they get depressed."

"I never knew with Candice. Sometimes I suspected she was seeing someone else, but I never had proof. It did bother me, I have to admit."

"Who would she turn to when she was down?"

"Her father. She hates her mother and adores her father." His laugh was not pleasant. "They're more than close. She used to call him from here when she was down and it would sound as if she were talking to her lover. If I were her mother . . ."

I saw nothing wrong there. We all need heroes.

"Did you ever meet him?"

"Once. He's a professor in Washington. He didn't take to me particularly. I can say the same for him. I think I reminded him too much of some other guy she got into trouble with."

"Trouble?" I leaned forward, eager and attentive.

"She wouldn't tell me. I figure it happened when she was around twenty. It was a disastrous relationship because of something she did. Look..."

"Any idea what she did?"

"No." He stood up and moved to sit nearer. "Why are we wasting time talking about her? You're a tourist here, aren't you? Let me show you the sights."

"That's sweet of you," having seen them already in the next room. "We might have dinner this evening. I'm staying at the Waldorf."

"Hey, that's great."

We stood up together and he took my unfinished drink.

"I'd imagine something like that disastrous relationship would really upset her."

"You must be kidding." He was clutching my elbow as if he'd just bought it. "She had to go to a shrink for a year. When she was with me, she was into some guru guy as well. It threw her way off base. Shook her confidence, you know what I mean?"

"Of course. Poor Candice."

He opened the door and I was back out in the corridor.

"I'll see you at, say, seven?"

"Smashing. And don't forget... the Waldorf."

On my ride out to LaGuardia I sat deep in the seat, sniffling a bit. The courage and resolve that had started me on the journey to Washington seemed to be somewhere around my ankles, like elastic-snapped knickers. Having sketched in my imagination a figure I could easily despise, I had believed—blindly—in my own fantasy. How could I have so underestimated David's tastes? He had chosen me; he couldn't have gone for less, only an equal or a better. So far she appeared, on the surface, marginally better.

I could imagine them, hand in hand, partners in a promising corporate empire, soaring up the stepping stones of success. I was the discarded bird, unable to match his pace and stride. Life, I was sure, did not flash past one's eyes at the moment of death, only at moments of despair. Mine looked as if it had reached a dead end, and I struggled to smother the feeling of futility.

On the flight, I dozed. Zooming around the world in the hunt was hardly the ideal occupation for a woman who hated traveling alone and felt the vulnerability of her sudden singlehood etching marks in her face and eyes.

It was pleasant in Washington. The green spaciousness of the city, after New York, reminded me of London and I felt a pang of homesickness. I passed familiar landmarks, recognizing them without having seen them except in pictures.

The taxi dropped me at the main administration center of the university, and I was directed, across campus, past all those lounging children on the grass to Dr. Schraft's office. He wasn't in, but his black chubby secretary allowed me to wait for him. She couldn't quite calculate who I was: certainly nothing academic. She wanted to "help"; I ignored her as she showed me into his office. It was a comfortable, solid room. There were books lining one wall, a window that looked in another, and one was covered with cork displaying haphazardly appended messages. I sat in a chair opposite a desk littered with papers and books—there was a pleasant chaos to the man—while the secretary fox-trotted uncertainly from one side to the other. She finally returned to her desk, leaving the door slightly ajar.

I had arrived in this office so quickly that I hadn't time to think of what I should say. The panic was rapidly spreading through my body. I turned my head and shifted around to look at the books. A blur of titles; I craned my neck until it hurt and then straightened painfully.

The desk looked slightly more promising. There was a manuscript, rubber-banded, in a tray. My eyes narrowed, then I had to smile: *An Existentialist Study of Shelley* by Eric Schraft. Beside it stood a silver frame of photographs.

I glanced toward the secretary, whose head was half-buried in a filing cabinet. I rose softly and edged toward the desk. The large color photograph was of a man with four women, all standing outside a house. One was obviously his wife and the others, I presumed, his daughters. They were blond and healthy. Which was mine?

I heard the outer door open and a whispered conversation. I was in my chair by the time Eric Schraft came in.

He turned out to be a portly bustling man, busy but susceptible to this stranger in his room. The small gray beard attached to his chin was a bit too neat and at times, when he spoke, he closed his eyes for too long. It was an affectation I didn't like.

"My name is Pauline Bell." How, after a lifetime of honesty, the lies rippled off my tongue!

He nodded, studying me. I could see the ticks and the crosses and the grades. He was, possibly, a handsome man; with that silly beard I couldn't tell.

"I was just visiting Washington, and Professor Yeats . . ." Yeats. The name from one of Charles's poetry books sprang up to fill in the blank. ". . . of All Souls suggested I look you up. I don't know anyone here and I'm tired of sightseeing."

"Yeats?" tapping his teeth, not hard enough to loosen the dentures.

"Alfred. I gather you two met at a seminar or whatever you professors have. He's an admirer of yours. A tallish man, narrow face and thick eyebrows," describing my father, minus the gray hair.

"Of course. How is he?"

"Not well. The gout, you know." An appropriate old

man's disease which I presumed afflicted American professors as well as British.

I should have had Irish blood in my veins. Instead, it was only Norman and Saxon with a touch of the ancestral rapist. For a few minutes we discussed Yeats, Alfred; a composite man who was part father, part uncles, part David. My eyes, however, kept sliding toward the photograph. Which was Candice?

"That's a lovely-looking family you have."

He reached for it, handed it to me. The proud father would surely reach into his wallet as well, wanting me to worship, as he did, the products of his phallus.

"Do you have any children?" he asked me.

"One, a boy." I studied the photo closely. "I'm separated at the moment."

"I'm afraid I only have daughters. I love them all, though. The two on the right are married, the one on the left," he hesitated, softening his voice, "Candice, is still single."

The photo was too small. I could only distinguish a coltish blond girl, half hidden in the shadows. Her breasts, in semi-profile, were attractive.

"She is the prettiest." The compliment, poisonous and bitter, seeped through my teeth.

"Don't tell the other two, but I think so as well. Candy and I are very close. I guess that's because she's the youngest and I brought her up. My wife died after Candy's birth." So Candy was burdened with two loves: hers as a child's, and her mother's.

"I married again, naturally. That's my second wife, Eileen."

"I thought they didn't look alike. How do they get on?"

It was not going to happen to me. Another man and David's children; or, and it would never happen, another woman and my children. If not for my own selfish reasons, then for theirs, they were not going to have a set of musical parents.

86

"Oh, fine. It's taken some time for Candy to get used to her mother, of course. She only knew me as father and mother for ten years. I'm afraid I spoilt her a bit but she's turned out into a fine woman. You should meet her when you return to New York."

"I'm only going to be passing through on my way back. But I'll certainly try." Which, of course, I wouldn't. I was confused enough with my names. There could be no introductions as Pauline Bell.

An Achilles heel, at least, was partly showing. A son needs a father to imitate; a daughter her mother. She would have more of the man than the woman in her, and that would be a flaw she could never quite overcome.

"That's a pity. She's a very clever woman, you know. She's started her own business and I know she's going to get to the top. I asked her . . ." He chuckled, to me it was only sad ". . . . when she was going to make her first million. Thirty, she said. She's twenty-five now. She really loved competing as a child. Instead of playing with other girls, she'd play softball or touch football. And does she hate losing!"

I filed that. Bad losers are vulnerable.

"Many girls do nowadays."

"Yes. She'll bust a gut to win—even as a kid she was like that. When she got older she learned how to do it differently. Like all women. And then the fellows really started lining up to date her."

The paternal pride overlaid the older man wanting what all men need, the elixir of youth and beauty beneath them as if a transfusion might take place somewhere in the middle of the ejaculation. I cannot understand them for that.

"I'm really surprised she didn't get married."

He hesitated too long, glanced once at the photograph, then said, "She did."

"Oh!"

Richmond hadn't mentioned marriage.

"She's divorced."

"I suppose marrying an older man does create problems."

"He wasn't older." This time, no glance at the photograph. He was studying *me*.

"I meant many women marry older men."

"Her husband was younger than she. It was a marriage in haste, didn't last more than six weeks. I hardly consider her as married then. Joey wasn't a man, just a boy. A very nice boy, hopelessly in love with her. I know she felt nothing for him."

"Then why on earth did she marry him?"

He glanced away, and it seemed as if a tremor disturbed the surface of his skin. When it passed the lines were deeper, the eyes hooded to hide the sudden glistening.

I felt a pain too, and looked down. My nails were deep in the palms of my hands; when I unclenched, moon scars remained.

"I suppose she thought she'd eventually fall in love with him. It happens sometimes."

"No. She never expected that. It was something that hurt her before."

"I'm sorry. What was it?"

"It happens."

He stopped abruptly and for a few moments I feared I'd been too openly and brutally inquisitive.

"She's a girl—a woman I suppose but for me she'll never grow up—who always leaps before she looks."

"Don't we all do that at times?"

"Candice does it too often. I think she wants desperately to be loved and to love. Her men always let her down."

If he could, I think he would have poured himself around Candice as a protective shield. All he could do, all any parent can do, was to sit helpless.

"Is she involved with anyone at the moment?"

"Yes, an Englishman as a matter of fact. It's another

one of her leaps. She wants this one to be permanent, but I suppose it depends on him. He left his wife, and those aren't the best of relationships. I told her that, but she's too happy enjoying the affair."

"Those can be very short."

"I know." He glanced at his watch and stood up abruptly.

"I'm sorry, I have to make a conference."

"And I have some sightseeing to do." I rose and he walked me out. "This relationship with the Englishman ... It could last a long time?"

"Possibly."

"Would you like her to marry him?"

"I don't imagine she's that inclined at the moment. The second time around is always more difficult, and I think she wants to get to know him a lot better. And, nowadays, very few young people want to get married."

"But would you advise it if she asked you?" We'd reached the corridor, and I was holding onto the doorknob for dear life.

"I'd say no. I'd like her to marry someone a bit younger and with fewer complications." He put out his hand. "Next time you're here, do give me a ring and come over to the house for dinner."

"I'd love that."

I felt him watching me as I walked down the corridor, my back stiff with knots.

She was nearer, now recognizable: her flesh materializing. I could feel it under my digging nails. I would need rest and thought before meeting her at the apartment tomorrow.

CHAPTER 6

IT WAS A GLOOMY DAY. THE CLOUDS THREW FAINT shadows across the park. An omen? I shivered and prepared for the confrontation, the ritual of bathing and exercising and dressing helped steady my nerves. The phone rang as I was penciling my eyebrows, and I finished with a line across my forehead. I stared at it for a minute, hoping it wasn't Candice postponing. I couldn't steel myself for another meeting; it had to be now. I was ready and primed, the violence as tight as a spring.

"Y-e-s?"

"It's Chapman." He sang out his name as if it were a trumpet to battle. "You sound very distant."

"What do you want, Chapman?"

"Lunch with you, Shelley. There's this place..."

"Thank you, Chapman. I can't."

"Dinner." He persisted as if he were in a race that had to be won. "I want to talk to you."

"Oh, all right." Though I doubted I would be in any condition to talk after this morning.

The breeze tugged at the yellow and brown scarf over my hair, sniffed the hem of my dress, touched, suggestively, the insides of my thighs. It was too short a distance for a taxi, but by the time I reached the apartment block I felt disheveled. The doorman opened the doors and I told him I was expecting my decorator in fifteen minutes.

I needed time alone: to prowl, to plot, to settle myself.

It was surprisingly light and airy in the apartment, as there were no curtains or furniture to anchor it down. I tidied myself in the bathroom, momentarily feeling the need to vomit as if I had morning sickness. I sat on the toilet until the feeling passed, gently kneading my stomach to relax the ball of nerves buried inside. I forced myself out of the sanctuary, and tried to walk, springily, around the rooms. I had to learn to play to this woman, to be giddy and excited and possessed of barrels of money and bad taste. Which was ironic, since if either of us were to furnish these rooms as we wished the result could be quite similar.

The buzzer sent what was left of my nerves into the pit of my belly. I panicked, not finding the intercom at first. Then, when it rang again, I traced it to the kitchen.

"Yes." The croak wouldn't travel far. "*Yes*?"

"A Miss Schraft to see you."

"Send her up, please."

I walked and stood at the window, not seeing Seventh Avenue below me. Outside this apartment, nothing existed. How long since I had first heard of her? Weeks, months, years? She was a lifetime to me.

I pulled my dark glasses out of my purse and slipped them on; my reflection looked silly in this dull weather. I took them off. Suppose she recognized me and walked out of the room? I put them on. I still looked silly. Finally I slammed the glasses back in the purse.

She had come. As the echo of the doorbell faded, I smiled and walked to the door. Father had said, in battle there is no time to be afraid; that fear only comes before and after. Death already lay behind me, now only the battle remained.

"Hello, I'm . . ." My hand was out, holding hers, pulling her in, and I'd forgotten my fucking name. ". . . Patricia." It sounded like "ShhPatricia" to me, but she didn't notice. I had my eyes on her face, her mouth, her eyes. "I'm so glad you could spare the time to look at this place with me."

"Oh god, I'm late, aren't I? I'm sorry." She dropped her bag and picked it up while she still talked in one rush of words. "Goddamned cabakazie driver took me up Central Park West and I didn't notice till we were on Sixty-seventh. I was trying to do my face. Never do that in a New York cab. Look . . ." She touched the smear of lipstick. "Where's the bathroom?"

I pointed and she was gone. I was glad. Her burst of fluster nearly had me stammering. I went to the window: the view might calm me as I organized my first impressions. A man, I supposed, would have to consider her very pretty. He would want to touch that full mouth and stroke the long, cool blond hair. Her skin was clear and taut with youth, but the blue eyes, fractionally too wide, appeared to reflect only the skimming of life. Transient lovers, no pain. They did not have the wary watchfulness around the edges.

She would never become a beautiful woman; she would remain a pretty one, creased and wrinkled but preserved for the rest of her life.

"What a fantastic view!"

She had come up behind me quietly, calmer and perfectly made up.

"Yes, it is."

"I have a friend who lives in Waterside Plaza on the thirty-seventh floor. One evening it was pouring and thundering and Paul decided to expose himself to the elements. So he stripped and went out on the balcony . . ." She began laughing and I noticed her dimples. I smiled, because she seemed happy. ". . . and said

'Here rain, here wind, here air . . . take me' . . . and the door slammed shut on him. He was stuck outside for two hours. If I had a place like this I think I'd do something like that. You're so lucky to have such space."

"Thank you."

We turned back to the room, which she now studied professionally. She pulled out a pad and scrambled deeper in her purse for a pen. It took a full minute to find one chewed pencil.

"Where do you live?"

"First and fifty-fourth. I used to live in a loft in the Village, but it got a little crowded. So when I started my business I figured I may as well move. It's not as good as this. In London I suppose this would be the equivalent of Belgravia."

I was glad she hadn't said Hampstead. As we moved from room to room, I wondered what the hell David had done with all the money. She didn't appear to have it. At least not the full amount, otherwise she'd be in a place like this. It was the kind of apartment David would have loved, at least for New York.

"Oh, I'm sure you'll be moving up." We went into the master bedroom. "I've been told so much about you . . ." She smiled, only ready for the caress of a compliment. ". . . and how good you are. I know you'll do a marvelous job."

"Why can't you do it yourself, Patricia?"

She studied my face a moment. I don't believe she'd really seen it until now. My stomach curled into a tight, expectant knot, but there was no recognition.

"I won't have the time, I'm afraid. I'll be having to return to London in a week or two, and these things take a lot of time if you want it done well. I feel I might be able to trust you to do it exactly the way I would."

We spent half an hour wandering from room to room. She sketched the rooms out roughly, and we talked like two old friends about carpets and drapes and chairs and beds. She did have, more or less, my instincts. I decided to abandon any stance of having bad taste.

"'Why don't we have lunch together?"

It was time to start becoming her friend. I had already chosen the restaurant. Expensive, impressive, and quiet enough so I could listen to her.

By the time we reached the Café in the Sherry-Netherland, we were both perspiring. The clouds only pressed the heat down on us; the breeze was too gentle now to give any relief.

Smoothed down and lightly powdered over, we took our table by the window looking out on Fifth Avenue. I smiled at Candice; she returned it and we conspired over what to drink and eat.

I leaned slightly forward, resting my chin in my palm and gazing at her as if she were a lover.

"Tell me more about your trip to England."

"It was one of the happiest times in my life." She was sipping her Bombay Gin martini. "To be honest, I can't remember very much. It was all a whirl. You know, shopping, the theater, the dinners . . ."

"Of course." And some of the time with my David, little dear.

"That's exactly what I do when I'm in London. Shop and theater. I don't get up there often, as I've been cloistered in Bristol for years. Did you only visit England on this trip, or . . ."

"I spent a week in Djerba. Do you know where that is?"

"No idea."

"That's an island off Tunisia. It's a beautiful place, just sand and sea. I was glad I went with a friend. In spite of him the Arab boys, especially the beach boys, treat a woman like a hooker. Especially a white one. I would never go there alone. I'd most probably end up in some horny sheik's harem."

I laughed and prayed that Allah would allow me that one wish.

"I've never been to the Middle East, Candice. This is the first time I've really done much traveling."

I wasn't going to hurry; gradually she would tell me what I would need to know.

She made it easy for me to know her. She was a friendly girl (I couldn't think of her as a woman); partly for the account I promised her, partly because she seemed to be genuinely wanting friendship. Over lunch—cold chicken with Chablis for me, steak poivre and Burgundy for her—she began by telling me about her sisters. Charlotte and Emily, after the Brontës; Candice after Candida. She didn't like either of their husbands.

When she made a face, her nose wrinkled attractively. "I don't know how they could marry men like that."

"There are women who do, as well you know."

"I suppose so, but Charly and Emmy were brought up in my family. I would have thought they would be more like me, or at least try to choose more interesting men. I want a man to be exciting, and I want to excite him. I want a relationship, not some kind of silent communion."

She did have taste. There wasn't a better choice, in my opinion, than David. My fists were clenched; glancing down, I saw I had slightly bent a teaspoon. I tried to straighten it, resting my hands on my lap, but didn't seem to have the strength. I dropped it, and kicked it under the table. Neither my eyes nor my smile wavered.

In return for her entertainment, I told her about debutante balls at the Grosvenor, drinking champagne on the lawns of Cambridge, punting down the Thames and falling in. Thank heaven for David: I had little doubt, with my tight circle of rich friends, that I would have ended up as one of them.

"It's been a marvelous lunch." I finished the coffee and we signaled for the check. "I can't remember when I've enjoyed myself so much. I know we're going to be such friends."

"Oh, I hope so."

"We will. Shall we meet on Monday at the apartment?"

"I should have my sketches ready by then."

I lay deep in the bathtub, hoping the steaming water would eventually loosen the knots in my back, thinking: blast, I could like the bitch.

CHAPTER 7

IN THE CHANDELIER GLOW OF THE RECEPTION HALL, Chapman looked wickedly handsome and elegant. Even in bed, I remembered, there was a permanent crease in his hair and moustache, and the chest hairs seemed to grow in a pattern. David could be a shambles at times.

"I don't want dinner, Chapman. Even a lettuce leaf would make me ill."

"You're not going to get out of our date that easily. Come on."

He led, I followed, out into the warm summer evening and toward the row of waiting carriages. I needed to be alone, yet I also wanted the diversion of company to escape the confines of the hunt. Chapman would have taken the first carriage; I chose a prettier one drawn by a big gray and handled by a girl.

"How about through the park?"

The girl glanced back at Chapman as the horse started off. "Not at this time of night, buddy."

We moved along Central Park. New York was no place for a horse and carriage, yet somehow the gentle swaying and the sharp crack of hooves comforted me.

It was nice to ride slowly and regally past the cars and people.

"Before we start, it's going to be no."

"Give it a chance, Shelley." He ignored his own irritation. "Look, I'm not going to give you that you-being-alone-me-being-alone line."

"You tried that one the other day."

"Apart from it not having worked a damn," he gave me a cheerful grin, "what the hell are you chasing this ... Tom ..."

"David."

"David for? Look, he's left you for this chick. How the hell do you think you're going to get him back?"

"I don't know."

"Did you meet her?"

I only nodded. I didn't want to talk about her.

"What's she like? Pretty, dumb, smart? Come on, Shelley."

"Pretty and smart."

"A tough combination. If she'd been dumb."

"David wouldn't have left with her."

The stupid pride of mine made Chapman raise a neat eyebrow. "So okay, he left you for a smart girl." He touched my hand and momentarily, weakened by the impact of his words, I allowed him to hold on. "'Let him go."

I couldn't see but shook my head stubbornly.

"You can't hold on to him forever, you've got your own life to lead and you have the children."

"They're no substitute at night, the darlings." I didn't mean just a sexual need, of course. It went beyond that: the touch, the feeling, the warmth, the sheer presence.

"He decided and you had nothing to do with it." In the pause a marriage slipped through his eyes. "The way Betty did for me. We think that our destinies are decided by God, or whatever, and at times of strength, even by ourselves. Bullshit. It's all decided for us by other people. Lovers, wives, children, parents—whoever we're fucking well depending upon. He's switched you onto another track, Shelley, and there's no way you're going to get back on the one he's on."

"I'm not a locomotive."

I was tired of truths, truths, truths. Homegrown or otherwise, practical or impractical. I was here to battle destiny, not meekly succumb because some idiot husband had run off with some idiot chick.

"In this situation, for all practical purposes you *are*."

"I was—thank God—never practical, Chapman."

If I were, I would never have married David, never have visited this awful city, never have stalked a totally strange woman, never have met Chapman. Practical people are the cul-de-sacs of human imagination.

"Why this touching interest in my welfare? I mean apart from . . ."

He bent his head, studied me. I sensed, I wasn't sure, that Chapman was about to make a revelation that I had no desire to hear.

"Why do you think I remembered you so well?" My shrug, I hoped, would make him veer. It didn't. "It wasn't because you screwed so well, Shelley. I've had them all, luv. When you race they come to you like lemmings falling off a cliff into the sea. They think they're giving their bodies as if it were the last fucking sacrament. You weren't one of them, you'd have had me even if I were a hotel busboy because it was me you went for, not some world champion. When you'd finished with me it was over, and I was the sucker that kept trying for you again." In this confidential mood he leaned toward me. "How many women do you think I've had?"

"One or two."

"I'm not trying to boast . . ."

"Oh, weren't you?"

"You know I wasn't. Look, I really had the most fantastic time during those two days we had. I don't mean the sex, sure you're good, but I just felt . . . happy."

"I am glad."

"If you'd stayed on, Shelley, I would have fallen in love with you."

There it came, despite my efforts. The stiletto of love, sliding in between the third and fourth ribs; no pain on its journey, just the sudden prick of panic. Oh dear God, how we all want to be loved and to love. We are so vulnerable to those words; the ultimate compliment, the blessing from above, the bloody miracle we never expect until it touches us; and then it becomes the burden that we doubt we have the strength to bear.

"Don't be silly."

"I'm being serious. But you'd prefer holding onto David, wouldn't you? He's your protection till death do you part." Brutally and sharply: "He's parted, luv."

"For a while." We turned down Park Avenue. I leaned out to peer at the Pan Am Building, straddling the street like an ugly colossus.

"Were you a virgin when you married him?"

"No." I didn't add that I had been one when we'd made love the first time. "And let's change the topic."

"You're scared of me, of knowing that David's fallen in love with someone else, of believing that you can love someone else. Hell, you're the one on the single track—David just switched his own direction. Instead of accepting it, finding another husband, another man anyway, you're chasing halfway round the world for this . . ." He would have been rude, but the muscles in my jaw warned him. ". . . fellow."

He studied me as I leaned back. I showed nothing and yet . . . This unexpected diversion from my preplanned destiny unsettled me. I hadn't expected it, in many ways didn't even believe his talk of love, and yet this feather-light promise held me suspended. Just so fractionally there wasn't even a perceptible change at that moment. I felt the attrition of my love for David.

He lay, maybe even at this moment, next to Candice in a bed.

"Why did Betty leave you?"

"Tired of waiting for my death, I guess. Then when I quit racing, I guess it was like lifting a rock off her back. None of the wives wanted to abandon a husband while he raced, y'know."

I didn't. "And so you let her go?"

"I couldn't hold her anymore. It was over, the waiting had been part of our love. Once it had gone, well . . ."

"But you were losing your races."

"That's the end of it anyway, luv. It's always the end when you stop trying to win."

I had been lying on the sand—bikini, sunglasses, scented lotion—orange juice in one hand, Proust, half open, in the other, cable, "DELAYED LOVE DAVID," stuck between the pages, and then I saw Chapman. Two days had passed since my arrival and I was half browned (I needed a week more to be fully cooked) and restless in the heat and the sea.

Monaco during the race week was a sight certainly worth missing: I hated cars and crowds. Chapman, with his neatly ironed swimming trunks, carefully combed hair, and a marvelous flat belly, was standing two feet away from me. If not looking down, at least half glancing, he feigned indifference.

"If you're going to pick me up, you better do it now." I closed the Proust with something like relief, and shaded my eyes up at him.

"British?"

"No, Hottentot." I shut my eyes, perhaps hoping he would disappear. The sand shifted beside me; he had sat down.

"So am I. English, I mean . . . Chapman Miles."

"How charming."

More sand moved and he stretched out beside me. I

was regretting my impulse, but he had staked out his territory.

"Listen, you're the one who asked me to pick you up."

"In a tantrum only."

"Well, I'm not leaving."

I let him stay, at first in silence and then, resigned, I encouraged fitful talk.

"I race," he said.

"You're too tall for that."

"What the hell has height got to do with driving a car?"

"I thought you meant horses. Too tall for a jockey. I don't actually like cars, you know. We give them too much attention. Now if you were a jockey I could talk to you about horses."

"I'm Chapman Miles." Never mind the noise, the name seemed to come out between closed lips.

"Yes, it must be unfortunate having a name like that." The announcement had little effect on me. I supposed he wanted my name, and I was reluctant to part with it.

"Chapman Miles won the championship last year. But I guess if you don't like cars you wouldn't know about things like that."

"I wouldn't." I stared out to sea, to the water flecked with tiny puffs of white and crowded with swimmers.

"I'm Shelley."

"Racing driver" was a new term in my vocabulary and I was feeling petulant about David's delay. Our holidays away from the children occurred only once a year, and I was missing him.

Chapman and I had lunch and, quite prepared to make him the total stranger when the time came, I allowed him to fondle my knees, my hands, my arms. To gaze deeply into my eyes. It wasn't to happen immediately; he had to test his car. The terrible noise of the motors forced me to retreat to the quiet of my room. He came, at six, supplied with champagne and the whiff of exhaust fumes.

Lovers for two days, never to meet again as far as I was concerned. I had abandoned myself, at least physically. We can afford to be brave in front of the stranger, but we must remind the stranger that he always will be just that. Now this "love" of his, germinating for years, a surprise to me, was back. Uncomfortably. The carriage stopped in front of the hotel and I silently followed him out into the street. He had thrown the stone, there was little more to be said, and now he waited for the ripples to reach me.

"Good-night, Chapman." I kissed him firmly on the cheek in front of half a dozen strangers and stepped into the elevator, having sensed his expectancy the moment we entered the hotel.

It was the silence, the waiting, that frightened me. Father had said that. How true. I have five days ahead of me, one hundred and twenty hours that, at times, simply refused to pass. I tried to squander those days; walking block after block in the heat, wanting to exhaust myself for the night, sightseeing around Manhattan, around the Statue, around and around and around, visiting the galleries, the movie houses, the theaters. Not only to escape the waiting but to avoid Chapman. And, of course, the telephone. It was so magical, so beautiful; each morning, as I rose, I would touch it. But if I picked it up, I knew I would dial her home and like some mute recorder wait to hear David say "Hello."

I thought of her, instead. How ironic that, friendless in this city, it was in Candice that I wanted to confide. In my effort to be her friend, I could feel myself slipping into becoming surely subconsciously just that. The need to hate, to hold that precise balance, was imperative. I had to hurl myself to the extreme of some variety of rage.

Anyone watching me might have been amused. At my face, sliding from coldness to passion, my lips muttering her name, murmuring his as I walked and saw and sat . . . I would watch lovers, and for some peculiar reason my eyes fell only on those who held hands. New York was full of them, all mocking my isolation.

Lying in bed watching the television during unaccustomed hours, I would find myself thinking about Chapman. I didn't want to believe him, to think myself capable of accepting his "love," yet I would not push his words out of my mind. Those words were so preferable to humiliation.

On the Monday, early, I phoned her home, and David said, "Hello." To me. I lay silently in the bed, the mouthpiece muffled, listening to him repeat the single beautiful word until his phone went dead.

Three hours later, pieced back together with lovely clothes and makeup, my resolution returned, wits collected, I telephoned Candice-at-work. My wooing was to begin again, at her office.

We met in the empty apartment, friends this time. She carried a large sketch pad. As we perched on the edge of the window sill, our heads together, almost touching, the two of us looking at her ideas for the rooms, I admired her. She was good, imaginative and stylish.

She dropped the pad on her lap, suddenly. The next I knew, her face was a few inches from mine.

"You think I look tired?"

"Not particularly."

"I should. I didn't sleep all night. I lost Frankie . . . my cat. He's the only survivor from my loft. I gave the others away, and he's been with me since he was a baby. At one in the morning I couldn't find him. We looked everywhere. I emptied the cupboards, the drawers, everything. I even ran around the street calling for him. I thought he'd fallen off the ledge."

"Cats can usually look after themselves."

"Frankie's like me. We both fall off carpets. I cried all night and then do you know where the bastard was? On the curtain rail. I gave him a one-hour lecture."

I picked the pad off her lap, sensing that she was going to continue talking about Frankie.

"You're very good," I said.

"Thank you." A faint crease appeared between her eyes. "I wish other people would take me on. I'm still waiting to be discovered." She stood, turned to the window and spread her arms wide. "Discover me, world!" She remained like that a moment, then slowly dropped her arms. Her smile was quick and shy. "No one ever listens."

"I'll tell all my friends in New York."

"That's sweet."

She turned and suddenly, before I could move, swooped and kissed my cheek. It was a gentle, innocent gesture, yet it burnt where her mouth had touched.

"You shouldn't have. I've done nothing yet."

Later, I opened my purse and gave her five hundred dollars in cash.

"I'd better give you a receipt." She solemnly wrote out a note and signed it with a flourish, grinning as she handed it to me and took the money. "Now I can go and have some formal note paper printed. Candice Schraft Inc."

"This'll do."

"Listen, if you're not doing anything now why don't you come to my health club? This is my keep-fit day. Tomorrow's my meditation day and Thursday's group therapy. I'm going to give that one up."

"I'd love to," I managed when she took a breath.

We caught a taxi and moved sluggishly through Fifth Avenue. As we passed Saks, she slunk down in her seat. "I always expect lightning to strike when I pass this corner. It's either going to come from the Church—I haven't been for years—or else a bolt is going to be hurled by Saks. I owe them a goddamned fortune."

"I'd bet on Saks. They'll have a better monitoring system than God."

The taxi pulled up in front of her health club on Forty-fourth Street.

"I don't have a leotard."

"I have a spare." She looked me up and down. "We're about the same size. You know, I'm so happy you said you'd come."

"So am I." She counted her change carefully, tipped the driver and got out.

"Do you live by yourself in New York? Apart from Frankie?"

"Oh no." So happily as she strode into the club. "I live with my lover."

I followed her into the reception area—all chrome potted plants and reclining chairs, with the ambiance of an expensive beauty salon. Candice signed me in and I handed over five dollars.

"I have a photograph of him."

"I'd love to see it."

She gave me the pad to hold, dived into her purse and pulled out a wallet of snapshots. My body felt like melting wax.

"There. That's David." She handed over the wallet. The glow in her voice—I refused to look into her face—should have, could have been mine. "He's English."

"Oh, he doesn't look it." I kept my head down, staring at the Kodachrome of my husband. If I met her eyes, she would have read the bitterness and recognition. "Though nowadays it's so hard to tell. I would have thought him American."

"He's always so English to me," craning to catch a

106

glimpse of the photograph, which I held tightly. She was standing with him, and their arms were around each other's waists; the background looked to be a pub somewhere along the Thames. "A strong face, don't you think?"

"He is . . . lovely."

We found ourselves in the changing room. The walls were pink, cutely feminine, with a row of mirrors along one side of the room. Four unappetizing women were remaking their faces. The rest of the room was taken up by small cubicles. Most of the women were middle-aged, more in need of miracles than exercise. Only one or two were as young as Candy.

"How did you meet him?"

"We met in New York last year." She took the wallet, glanced at the snapshot and dropped it back in her purse. "He was here to set up a deal for his toy firm, and a friend introduced us. Wow! He really knows how to sweep a woman off her feet. He was so sure he wanted me."

"The photograph looks as if it was taken in London." If I smiled, would my face crack?

She took my purse, dropped it with hers in the locker, and handed me the black leotard. We chose booths next to each other, so we could talk and change at the same time. I could hear her clothes rustling as I stripped quickly.

"We kept in touch, and when I went to London I looked him up. We had a glorious two weeks together." She stopped for a moment; I hoped from guilt choking her. "Not the whole time, though."

"Why not?"

"He's married."

"Ohhh!" A long sympathetic note, full of understanding and compassion. No doubt a talent picked up from my mother, though I never did have her complete range of expression. Practice would help, no doubt. "Did you know it when you met him?"

"Yes. He told me he was very happy with her, too."

The pleasure and the puzzlement intoxicated, then flattened me. He was happy, and I was fulfilled but, my god, what more does a man want than to be happy? Did he leave because he'd been too happy—was that possible? Or in between his telling her and his leaving, had the happiness run out?

"It's strange that he should have left her then, if he was happy."

My voice was so distant that I seemed only to hear an echo. "Her," meaning me. Curious that I could call myself that, could stop myself from rephrasing the question to: Why did he leave *me*?

"That was when we first met. Things had changed some by the time I visited London."

How long was that? One year, nine months? Time enough for the universe to change, and yet my mind, racing backward, forward, ferreting, discarding, longing, couldn't discover this change. It had taken place outside my vision. She had to know the reason, but I cringed from the knowledge. I wanted to hold it off just that while longer, to give me time to build up my strength.

We both stepped out of our cubicles at the same time.

"Did you ever meet her?" It had to come. A natural question to which I thought I already knew the answer.

Candice studied me. "Yes. In a way." She half smiled, the perfect teeth glistening in the light. "I've seen a picture of her."

CHAPTER

8

THE HEART DOES STOP. SO DOES THE BREATH. THE body, all bone and flesh and blood, does become unbearably heavy. I saw those huge blue eyes that seemed to fill her whole watchful, calculating face. I felt, suddenly, fear of her—and despair for myself.

She had known about me from the very moment I had entered her life, and I, so absorbed in my own cleverness, hadn't thought beyond the stalking of her. She circled me: watchful, waiting until this moment. What did Father tell me? "I attacked once and the blighters weren't there." He had been lucky; I was surrounded.

"Oh," I heard myself: short and sweet.

She laughed and pushed back her hair. "She's quite lovely, but it's hard to tell."

I grasped the "she"; held onto it with all my nerve.

"Why? Is the photograph blurred?"

"Oh, it's not a photograph. David has a painting. A smallish one . . ." She measured out the size of my self-portrait with her hands. A foot by a foot, if I remembered correctly, and for sheer relief, I laughed aloud. She looked puzzled and I shook my head at the private joke. ". . . done in oils. It's not really very good, a bad imitation of Van Gogh. She's supposed to have done it in college and I told David it was a good thing he married her. She'd never have made it as a painter."

"Is it hanging in the bedroom?" The elation spiraled, glided, hoisting me higher and higher so that it seemed as if I was looking down on her from a great height.

Her angry snort only lifted me even higher. He had wanted to, she said. "I told him he'd better keep it locked in his briefcase. If it had been a good painting I wouldn't have minded—well, not too much. But it's awful."

My grin must have looked silly; she could have called the painting atrocious, me ugly, and I would have smiled. David held on to me, still, recalling me as a young woman.

The gym was large, airy and too bright. Men and women were grunting, sweating, pounding their bodies against machines. The men, on an average, looked fitter and slimmer; the women worked harder. Candice and I took bicycles next to each other, mounted and pedaled.

"Was David . . ." Oh god, *has* she mentioned his name? ". . . your first lover?"

"No." Not noticing the pause. She seemed to sigh; it could have been her effort on the machine. "I fell madly in love when I was twenty. The guy was forty-eight—I seem to make a habit of older men. I'd just finished college and moved to New York when I met him at work. He was a director of the company, a brokerage, and he had five seats on the exchange. He was everything a girl that age dreams about. Handsome, dashing, rich, and a marvelous lover. There was one thing I didn't want. He was married."

"You seem to make a habit of that, too."

"Right, that's me. I pick the wrong man, unerring.

David's going to be different." She pedaled harder, and I tried my best to keep up with her. She seemed to be trying to work out the pain, still there hidden where she hoped she'd never find it. "Anyway, Bob—that was his name—and I made the scene together. There was his apartment on Fifty-eighth Street, he helped, and he moved some of his stuff in . . . a couple of suits, shoes. Enough to keep me ecstatic. We'd have dinner two nights a week, and a couple of weekends we'd go down to Acapulco or Key West . . . it was like heaven. God, I really loved him."

Her eyes were closed. I glanced away, the way we do when we want to give a friend, even a stranger, privacy from our eyes. Across the room, a chubby man ran endlessly on a machine in front of a mirror.

"Patricia, have you ever loved any man so much that it hurts?"

"Yes."

"I never realized it could be like that. When he began seeing me less, it became worse. We'd been dating—funny word—a couple of years, then he was talking marriage. That was all I wanted. I guess when he said that, I became more possessive. I wanted to see him every day. Of course he couldn't. He had a wife and four kids in Westchester—but we were going to run away to some paradise island. I don't know when it began to happen. From twice a week it dropped to once a week, then once every two weeks. I was going mad and that's when I did a stupid thing."

She stopped pedaling, her head up and back, sucking in air with a greedy open mouth, and sweat, like tears, trickled down her face. Flushed, glowing, she was touchingly pretty; her nipples extended, the breasts firm and high, her legs long and well muscled.

"What?" I dismounted and move away.

She followed. I could smell her perspiration and her perfume.

"I got myself pregnant by him." Her laugh was flat,

harsh. "My father always told me I'd do anything to win . . . even dumb things, and this was the dumbest. But I just couldn't think of anything else to hold him."

"I am sorry."

"Hell, getting pregnant was the easy part."

She began exercising in the open space. I stood opposite and touched my toes in time with her.

"He reacted like a perfect gentleman. He came to the apartment, handed me an envelope of cash—with a kiss, naturally—and left me to my abortion. I never saw him again."

"Bastard."

"Yes. I still can't blame him, though. I was old enough to look after myself." She touched her toes a dozen times. Thankfully I could too. She sat, legs together, outstretched.

"Could you hold my ankles?"

I did, watching her lie back and sit up smoothly, effortlessly.

"The only person I could really turn to was my father. He was a real darling. I think it hurt him as much as it did me. I couldn't tell my stepmother . . . we don't get on well together. He took me to the clinic, waited for me and looked after me for a couple of days. He wanted to stay longer, or else have me back home. I was going to be the brave girl, and I wouldn't let him stay. I wish I had."

"You didn't do anything . . . silly, did you?"

"Don't look so worried. Not that silly. Your turn."

She sat up, held my ankles and watched me lie back and rise. I wasn't about to do as many as she had. "There was a guy from school I knew who was sweet to me. An all-American kid, if you know what that means. The boy next door. He began dating me, and . . . I don't know. It was just wanting to be wanted, after all I'd been through. I married him."

"Oh, dear."

"I know." She was studying me, critically. "When I'm your age I hope I have as good a body as yours."

"Thank you, Candice. I think I've had enough now."

I sat, next to her, puffing. Her face suddenly looked older, wiser. She hadn't skimmed, as I'd guessed earlier, but had dipped, and deep. I wished . . . I didn't have to push her deeper. I wished she was another person. That woman across the room.

"How long did it last?"

"A couple of weeks . . . He was hurt by what I did, but I couldn't survive in the marriage. I didn't even try. You can't keep thinking of other people, can you?"

"No."

"Want to swim? I spend half an hour in the pool. It's the best exercise." I had regained some breath as we strolled out of the gym which reminded me so much of my schooldays.

"I don't think so. But you go ahead. I wouldn't mind a sauna, if they have one." I needed to be alone to attain, once more, some distance.

"Oh, I'll join you."

There were three women, baking, sweating, wrapped in towels and perched on the tiers like miserable pigeons.

"Does David know all this?"

"Not all. He knows about Bob but not about the abortion or the marriage. I'll tell him later."

I weighed the precious information carefully. It's never wise to hide your past from a lover, no matter how trivial; and this wasn't trivial.

"Do you think I should tell him?"

"It's hard to say without knowing him, but I suppose you should."

David would have to be told, but not by me. It would have to be another person. If not Candice, then who? In the heat, I couldn't think of anyone.

"I'm surprised you didn't go into analysis over that. I would have."

"I did for a while. Until I found Pete."

"He's not another cat, is he?"

She bumped into me as she laughed. Her skin was silky and hot.

"No. He's my psychic. He's so tuned into me, Patricia. I swear he knows my whole life. He told me I was insecure with women because I never had a mother... He says I'm very ambitious and I'll succeed. In fact," she stared at me and wiped the sweat off her face, "he told me last month I'd be having a relationship with a woman. Oh, nothing sexual..." She giggled.

I smiled. "Was it to be a good relationship?"

"Pete wasn't sure. He couldn't see properly... he just felt that we might get on. He told me about David and how we'd meet long before it happened."

"Did he say it would last?"

"Oh, forever." She glanced at me speculatively. "I'm always talking about myself. You must be bored stiff."

"Not at all. I find you fascinating. No psychics in my life... or lovers at the moment."

"I don't even know if you've been married."

"Was. I'm separated now. I found out that my husband was..." Think, Shelley, think. "... queer. Over here you call it gay."

"Didn't you know when you married him? I would have."

"Not with an Englishman."

To be cuckolded not by a woman but by a man was, presumably, a common humiliation these days. Closets have become revolving doors. I tried to imagine the moment of revelation for Patricia Middleton, discovering her husband mooning over a young boy's magnificent ass. Maybe even returning home from the supermarket to find the two of them grappling into her pillow. The shock, the hysterics, the accusations of infidelity.

"I suspected it when he came back smelling of Aramis. He always used Monsieur Lanvin."

"What a coincidence." She laughed and clapped her hands. "That's the same after-shave David uses."

"Is it?" I smiled. "I didn't exactly catch them flagrante delicto. We discussed it all very sensibly—he said he preferred men, and I said 'Oh.' And that ended that."

I sighed. It was arduous concocting a story and remembering it in this 120 degree heat. I was hoping she'd had enough.

She had. We both rose, slippery with sweat, and went to adjacent showers. She got me a cap, and the water, cool and hard, silenced us both. I needed the silence. She was ready—stretched, opened, vulnerable—for my incision. If I could do it without wounding her further, I would, but I didn't know how. I didn't even know as yet how to use what I knew. It was going to take more time, more waiting.

Dried, wrapped in towels both soft and large, our shoulders touching, we strolled back to our cubicles to change.

"When did you decide that David was the man you wanted?"

"After our time in New York. He's such a strong gentle man, sure of himself . . . And you know, he's one of the few honest men I've met. So when I had enough money I made the trip to London, and the first person I phoned was him."

And so, giving me no warning, she descended out of the skies, a vampire to suck at my heart.

"Haven't you felt any remorse?" That almost medieval word; far superior to "guilt," which implies crime and not emotion. "For breaking up his marriage?"

"I don't think his marriage was working. I'm quite happy to have him. I suppose I should have some feeling for Shelley, but she wasn't his type, you know."

"Oh?" I suppressed all impatience to demand why. It was a game. I was the stranger to this person Shelley, I had to work the information out inch by agonizing inch. I felt no pain, only an almost calm, lunatic detachment.

"How long were David and Shelley married?"

"Eighteen years."

She could have as easily said eighteen days or eighteen hours. It meant nothing to her. My past was not hers; she could be indifferent to this wretched woman—tearing her hair out in suburban Hampstead, sending frantic pleas to her husband, cursing the mercenary bitch who had robbed her—named Shelley.

"I thought about her a lot, imagined her the best I could. Finally I decided I didn't like her very much."

We took chairs next to each other in front of the overlit mirrors. I could have done with more shadows; next to her framed face, without makeup, I felt like a crone. There was one other woman in the rear carefully leaning forward, at the far end, painting her eyelids. No one, as this acre of pain spread through my chest, to reach for.

"Want to try this? It's my favorite."

She gave me her perfume; I put it on my wrist and sniffed. It was delicate, L'Air du Temps, pretty and too young for me.

"It's lovely. Why don't you like her? Shelley, I mean."

The question had come like a child out of my body. She was to answer me at any moment with a vision not as she saw me, but as David did.

The wait was interminable as she frowned, summing me up into one single image as if I were a black and white photograph or a waxen doll. I wished I were kneeling and protected by the soaring arches of a silent cathedral.

"Arrogant."

Candice's one-word summation of Shelley drove the

breath out of me and I snapped the clasp of my necklace. "What a shame," she said, but she was nodding to herself, obviously satisifed with her thrust at this stranger.

Me? Arrogant? The mirror other people hold up for our reflection is seldom the one we want to look at.

"Is that what David says of this . . . Shelley?"

"No, but that's the impression I get. He talks about her with a sort of . . . well . . . awe. I don't think he's ever gotten over the fact that he feels that she's better than him. She's an aristocrat, a general's daughter, knows a Monet from a Manet . . ." Her sniff was disdainful. ". . . and who the hell doesn't, adores Artur Rubenstein and all that bullshit. He talks of her as if she's this goddamned goddess. I told him he was nuts. I said you fuck her, don't you? So how can you keep thinking of her as this when she's flat on her back?"

A ruined room in a London slum eighteen years ago should have disillusioned him. And yet, don't we, who create the heroes, forget who first fashioned them?

"What a bloody fool!"

"That's what I said as well."

"Why on earth did he marry her?"

"David's ambitious and she had what he wanted. Style and class."

"But he did love her?"

Had I loved eighteen years, into nineteen this year, only to discover through a stranger that there was none returned?

Her shrug was evasive.

"I suppose so, it's difficult to say. Sometimes he seems to have loved her and other times . . ."

That was enough for me. "Sometimes" is the most one can demand of love, which can never be constant. No one is strong enough to generate that same energy day in and day out, month after month, year after year. I had my "sometimes" when for days and weeks I could feel nothing for him; an indifferent calm would prevail between us and I would be enclosed in a hopeless solitariness. Then a gesture, a word, a glance would awaken the love again. She would not be able to understand that. In the middle of passion, she could not see the end of it ahead of her.

"Do you have the style and class, isn't that what you called it, he wants?" I finished my face and watched her brush her lashes.

"Not as much as she does. In a way I think . . ." She glanced at me. ". . . she would be somewhat like you. You're the sort of person I imagine this Shelley would be, though you are much nicer. I feel she's a very aloof person. A snob, really."

"Even though she married David?"

"In spite of that. I guess she fell in love with him, but don't forget he became pretty rich. If he'd stayed a factory worker or whatever, the marriage would never have worked."

"But he had been . . ." Wait—I knew nothing about Shelley. ". . . weren't they poor at the beginning?"

"Of course, but she knew he wouldn't remain poor."

"You make her sound very calculating."

"I think she is."

"She does sound awful." We got up together and went out.

"Is that why he left her?" It would have to be the last question about these two strangers, David and Shelley, for Candice was looking at me thoughtfully.

"Partly, though it's hard to tell. I think he wanted a new challenge and she didn't want to go along with him. She was safe and secure in her little house. With me he knows there'll always be a challenge. I'm not going to be a bloody hausfrau the way she was."

Arrogant, calculating, boring. That, according to Candice, was Shelley, and it depressed me into silence. To be all of that was enough to drive any man out of a marriage. And Candice, healthy and pretty, filled with love and life, was the alternative. I could have given him more but even now I couldn't see how I would be able to divide myself any further between him, the three children and myself. There just wasn't enough strength to go around in any woman.

"You're thoughtful, Patricia."

"I was thinking how romantic it all is. Why did he fall in love with you?"

"My face bones, he said." She turned and laughed so I could see them. They were more pronounced than mine. "He said he'd never ever met such a daft bird with beautiful bones. How could I resist that? At first when he said 'daft,' I thought he meant draft, and I just couldn't figure it out. It means nutsy, doesn't it?"

"Yes."

"Well, when a woman gets that kind of compliment, and he also said someone like me needed looking after ... The only thing I could think of was to go to London and get him."

"I guess he was flattered."

"Oh yes."

I doubted whether I could take any more. It felt as if the knife had turned and I was the one who'd been gutted.

"I want to get my necklace fixed, Candice, so ..."

"Oh, you should see Anne. She's my best friend." She wrote Anne's name down and gave the paper to me. "She runs a fabulous little jewelry shop on Fifty-eighth Street. Be sure to mention my name."

"I will."

She stopped and faced me. We were two feet apart and the crowds flowed around us. I sensed another confidence and tried an encouraging smile. I only hoped that if "Shelley" was to be stabbed once more I would be able to hold the muscles of my face in this interested, attentive expression.

"I wasn't sure whether I liked you in the beginning," she said. "You seemed like another one of those rich women I meet constantly in my job and always hate. All money and no taste. You've got to jump to their bidding, yes ma'am, no ma'am, and the things they choose . . ." She winced and laughed. I laughed too; she was now emotionally committed to me. "But you're so nice, and I think you're genuinely interested in me."

"Oh I am, very much. When I met you I felt quite certain we'd be friends."

"We are, Patricia." She strayed a couple of feet away. "Why don't you come and meet David? His office is next to mine." She took my arm and gently pulled as I tried to stay rooted to my spot. "I'm sure you'll like him."

"I already do . . ." I gently removed my arm from her grip. ". . . from what you've told me. I have a four o'clock appointment but I'd really love to meet him. Let's make it a foursome after you've done the apartment."

"Do you have someone special in New York?"

"More or less."

"I wish I had your assurance sometimes."

"I don't think it would suit you, Candice." I had to remove the barb before it bit too deep. "It's only a facade, you know."

My appointment was with the hotel room. I sat, feet up on the air-conditioner, staring out over Central Park. I was buried up to my neck in the ashes of her words, and unable to rise out of them.

In that sorry room eighteen years ago I had made certain calculations. Until then I'd only had worshippers who fumbled with my body and were repelled by my strength. (My arrogance, I suppose, in Candice's terms.) David had taken me that night the way I needed to be taken; overwhelmed by someone stronger. Don't we all calculate our future, whether we're alone or not? I'd had faith that David would be the success that he wanted to be by forty. Had he not succeeded, our marriage would indeed have dissolved—not for lack of money but because of his sense of failure.

I was a housewife. I had chosen the role, not had it thrust on me. I never fantasized myself as the tycoon of the family—a Chagall or a Modigliani, perhaps, though I knew the talent was not there. I had worked for the first two years of our marriage as a book-jacket designer, creating melodramatic covers for mediocre books. It was a job that would have depleted all my enthusiasm for life had I remained at it for long.

Instead, never attracted by the ritual of daily labor, I happily practiced the art of being a wife and mother, and grew in the adventure of marriage and children. Charles, Samantha and Miranda would grow as strong and secure as were David and I, and nothing else had mattered.

At seven o'clock the telephone rang. It was a relief to escape from the brooding; this time I was happy to hear Chapman's voice.

At seven-thirty he sent flowers, a bouquet of lilacs. Vulnerable to romantic gestures, I spent longer than usual preparing myself for our dinner. The flowers lightened my mood. I hummed, sang, even danced between bathroom and dresser. It had been decades since I'd been courted, and though I didn't want that, it gave me a new confidence.

When I swirled into the bar, I sensed the looks. I felt as wispy as the ankle-length dress that floated and whispered around me.

"Chapman!" An arm around his neck and a kiss, gentle but firm, slightly above his mouth. He had wanted to kiss my mouth, but I was quicker.

"Delicious." His hand was on my waist and the faint surprise slipped off his face. "Why the sudden affection?"

"I feel like it." I pushed his drink toward him. "Finish it. I want to go somewhere high above the city."

"I could arrange a helicopter ride."

"Has it got a bar?"

"No."

"Then I'll have it later. First a few drinks to get me halfway up there."

"Why do you 'feel like it'?" We moved out past the still fountain outside the hotel, I clinging to his arm.

"Stop dissecting my mood as if I were a frog. Just let's have a good time."

"Like lovers?"

"Who've never met before."

"Or who met already once years ago?"

"Maybe, Chapman, I don't know."

"And one of them gets shoved off the roof again?"

"Someone always does, Chapman." I felt the contraction in his arm. "And then again, maybe they don't. Where are you taking me?"

"Do you care?"

"I don't, as long as it's high up. And of course it has to have a bar."

"The Rainbow Room overlooked pink, twilit haze. It hung outside the window like a gas, hovering close enough to attack the inhabitants of this glass-enclosed bowl.

"Pollution."

I had wanted to look out across Manhattan, to see the lights and the avenues stretching out like a backdrop.

"Let's change seats, Chapman. I don't want to look at it."

We crossed over, brushing hands. This time, when I sat facing the wall and him, I allowed him to keep my hand. I wanted not to recall Monaco but to remember what it was like to be a lover again. To be wooed, touched, gazed at. To flirt!

"You are handsome tonight." Only his ex-wife would know what he looked like at dawn after years of marriage. "You always are. I wonder how many women have told you that?"

122

"Not one the way you do." He kissed the inside of my palm. If he had kissed the wrist, he would have smelt the perfume. "They may say it but they don't make me feel it. You're looking magnificently beautiful, like a woman in love. I hope you are."

"I always have been. How many times have you been in love? Countless?"

"No." I waited for his answer as we ordered our drinks. It was a pleasant room, not exactly memorable except for the view. It felt timeless, peaceless. It would feel the same, maybe even with the same waiter, on top of the Nile Hilton or the Euromast in Rotterdam.

"I think only three times that I could count as love," said Chapman. "Betty was the long-term one. There were two short and passionate ones. Monique, a French painter, and . . ." He nodded in my direction.

"Was Monique like me? I mean, was it a weekend?"

"It lasted four and a half months. I even left Betty for her once." He looked over my shoulder as if she were alive and rising out of the haze. I couldn't tell in which way he regretted the decision, leaving his wife or returning to her. "Monique was doing a series of paintings for one of the big French magazines when we met. It was the Berlin Grand Prix and I was second to Jimmy Clark in the world championships. He won in Berlin and clinched it. Monique was small and had a very sensual French face. It started off as a one-night stand and then . . . Christ! It was like being drained and drowned at the same time.

"There must be as many different ways of loving as there are of dying. Betty was a calm, quiet love—with Monique it was jumping into the fire together. We were either fucking, fighting or loving each other. She was jealous of my cars and my wife. I was jealous of her work and her past lovers. We had a sort of total greed for each other. I couldn't see enough of her and after the race in Amsterdam I decided I was going to live with her. It was insane. I knew it wouldn't last, and it didn't."

"What did Betty do when you left?"

"Sat and waited." He sounded disappointed still after all these years. "As if I were in just another race. When I came back it lasted about a month longer and by then we were both burnt out—Betty just said 'I hope you've got it out of your system' or something bloody trite. I nearly left her again."

"Why? What did you want from her? Blood and tears?"

"To be needed. And missed."

"And what would I have been? Another Monique?"

"We'll never know, will we?" His fingers, caressing my pulse, managed to raise its rate by a couple of beats. "Unless you change your mind."

Over the rim of my glass I watched him watching me. He was still caressing my hand, murmuring on about my beauty. I purred.

"What about you?" He edged his chair around nearer to me. The table was small enough but the chairs were too deep. "Apart from this David."

He always made the "David" sound somewhat derisive. I decided not to take offense.

"There was you."

"Come on, Shelley." He worked his way up my forearm; I removed it out of reach, by facing him. "I was only a screw to you. I mean being in love with someone other than your husband."

"What's wrong with loving only your husband? You make it sound like an attack of gangrene."

"Nothing."

That sounded as if I'd died. My epitaph: Here lies Shelley who loved only one man. Poor thing. A few love affairs, half a dozen I suppose would be a nice round number, would have made more of a woman of me. Unfortunately I felt that he was succeeding in making me feel inadequate. Just fucking wasn't going to be enough; demonic loving was the only way to satisfy him.

"There was Sean."

He was a skinny poet who claimed kinship, through the bottle, to Dylan and Behan. His poetry was pretentious—though at the time, for the weekend, I thought him a genius. I certainly hadn't loved him; even liking had been something of a strain. We met at a weekend house party in Cheshire. David was away on a business trip to Japan, and I had the children with me.

Sean was a dazzling figure: velvet waistcoat, his hair in ringlets, a gold earring in his left lobe. He also wore a drooping moustache and a permanent, hazy smile. The children, clinging to my skirts all day, failed to deter him as I was the only manless woman around. He flirted over their heads, patting them when they began to pay too much attention to his words, and even offering Charles, aged ten, a beer.

Sean's book of poems had been well reviewed, largely thanks to the critics' fondness for making "discoveries" from time to time. His poetry had been read on one of the more obscure television programs. Over dinner, with a dozen whiskies and beers in his stomach and that Gaelic tongue flapping furiously in the wind, he whispered about the wild Irish beauty in my eyes and my mouth and my hair. He saw enough streams and stars and rainbows to make me feel like a poetic landscape. I hadn't the heart to tell him it was wasted on me; I had decided while dressing for dinner to allow him to seduce me. The words were heady; for sure, they were pretty lies.

He had come to my room at midnight, wearing a red silk dressing gown that fell to his knees, a glass of brandy in his hand. He was a man who would be lowered into his casket with his fingers permanently curled. Priorities: he put the glass down reverently, then knelt and kissed my hand, my bare shoulder, finally my mouth. His mouth continued its whispering but I couldn't distinguish a word. His kiss tasted of toothpaste and brandy. He opened his dressing gown: he had a child's body with a man's belly and an erection full of promise.

"You're a beautiful lass. Beautiful."

The covers were off, a sip of brandy, another sip, then he was beside me. A few more kisses and he was inside. He began enthusiastically and then quite suddenly, sighing, he laid his hand on my shoulder and the weight of his body settled on mine. I waited, expectant.

"Sean!" I stroked his head. He didn't stir, only snored.

A half fuck and it was over.

I laughed aloud.

"What is it?"

"Just a funny thought. I was more a romantic love, I suppose. He was a poet and such a beautiful man. At the time I thought he looked like Byron. He'd write me sonnets. Silly and schoolgirlish but it was marvelous. The affair lasted . . . six and a half months. We used to make love in his apartment in Notting Hill. He wanted me to run away with him but I couldn't leave the children. So . . ." I shrugged as expressively and with as much sorrow as could be summoned. A woman just entering the room distracted me. She was beautiful and wore a marvelous silk print blouse. "I wonder where she bought that?"

Chapman swiveled, studied the woman rather than the blouse, then returned his attention to me.

"It's surprising how quickly we forget all about it. I thought the pain of Monique and Betty would last forever. It didn't, and I wonder why."

"Survival." Given time I had no doubt I would— with or without another man. I had made the choice of wanting to do that with David. "Isn't there a higher place we can go to?"

126

We reached the pad by the river just minutes before the helicopter was to take off. When it did, I screamed and held like death and was not feeling that buoyant. My spirit for adventure was being used up too quickly for my liking. When I tried to release my hand, Chapman ignored the wriggling efforts; I gave up, tagging along meekly to the restaurant he'd chosen.

"Betty wouldn't have screamed." There was a slight note of irritation behind the smile.

"David knows I always scream, and I have no intention of changing the pitch for you. I don't like flying in small planes."

"Betty used to fly mine when I was too tired after a race. I have a Comanche because it's the quickest—was the quickest, I should say—way to get around Europe."

"Well, David never needed to get around Europe that fast, nor did I. I can just about manage a car if I'm the only one allowed to panic."

"I don't like anyone driving me." He chewed thoughtfully on the meat as if he had me in his mouth. Was he calculating the prospect of a future with a woman who screamed? "I guess that's because of my profession. I always want the wheel in my hands, at least I used to. Now that I've stopped driving I've changed in quite a few ways."

"You miss it?"

"Oh god, yes." The lines around his mouth were deep with the longing for lost power. It was enough for me to want to cradle him; touch the lines and magically erase them. "I spent twenty-five years in it, luv, and—winning or losing—it was like nothing else on earth. When you're driving you're so close to life. Not death. Both on and off the track. There's so much intensity in everything you do, that . . . it's like nothing else."

"I've never lived my life like that. Few people can, I suppose. Children, house, husband . . . if you start getting too intense with them you'll all have a nervous breakdown. I try it in peaks. Loving, being very happy, being very sad. But the rest is all a plateau, with the morning papers and the goodnight kiss." I refused to feel guilty for the calm and quiet of my life—I had never wanted much more out of it. That may have been my mistake. Lack of ambition.

"Betty used to travel with me. She loved racing though she hated me driving. France, Germany, Spain, South Africa, America. Once the kids were old enough, we'd leave them behind. I think by the end she knew as much about Formula cars as I did."

"Didn't she ever get lonely chasing around with you? I would have hated it."

"There were the other wives."

"That's no compensation for a woman."

"They all knew each other and stuck together."

"While you raced and screwed?"

He laughed, even as he must have when Betty was with him. Men make such misjudgments about their wives. "She didn't mind. They all knew we didn't care a damn for the chicks we had on the circuit."

"I'll bet she minded all the same."

I did about David's women, though I managed to accept that it would happen. There's always some bitch wanting what you have. And the flattery of sliding into another wanting body is too much for a man to resist.

"Maybe. Anyway, that's all in the past." He touched my hand gently to hint that I could be the future. "You'll come with me to Watkins Glen, won't you? Please, Shelley."

"I've got to think about it."

"That's enough for me." He smiled, happy with my retreat from a firm "no."

It was cool and wonderfully pleasant outside. We held hands and walked slowly, stopping to look into windows. It was another world, distant from David and Candice and the children. I was Chapman's stranger once again, and I wanted it to be that way forever. We reached the hotel too soon. I needed to have walked another few blocks to make up my mind; I knew what we were both wanting.

My floor was first, and Chapman stepped out with me. The doors closed and we were alone in the long silent corridor. Chapman didn't ask or wait. He turned me around, touched my face, kissed my mouth.

"I do love you, Shelley."

"I know."

"Forget about David. Marry me."

I kissed him back, unable to do more. I had meant to say things but there was no way and no time to pick a path through the mined jumble of my thoughts. This night would mean not just an orgasm but listening to him murmuring his love; maybe even believing him. Those whispers were the lever that would widen the gap between David and me.

"Why not?" He camouflaged his impatience by kissing my ears while his fingers explored the catch on my bra. "I do love—"

"Don't keep saying that, Chapman. Please." I disentangled myself and walked down the corridor, keeping his hand.

"I mean it."

"I do know, and that means something to me. But *really*, Chapman." I could see that the future, so strong and resolved before I had met Chapman this time, was something that could dissolve the moment I reached it. "And there's David."

"Fuck David."

If only he knew how much I wanted to.

"He's my husband."

We reached my door; he took the key and slid it into the lock. "We're not two strangers in Monaco, are we?"

"No. It's my fault." I turned, the door opening behind me, and glimpsed the folded-down covers of the bed. "I wanted to be romantic tonight. That was the mood I was in. Give me time, Chapman."

"I won't mention it again, until you're ready to hear it." He looked past my shoulder. "May I come in?"

"I'm having my period." A half-lie as it was nearly over, but few men want our blood on their precious bodies.

"I don't mind."

"I do. I can't enjoy myself." All those towels underneath, though there had been countless times that I'd tolerated it out of my need for David.

He smiled and inclined his head. The smile only moved a corner of his mouth but it was complete with understanding. How many times had Betty told him that? I doubted he had heard the excuse from many other women. Maybe Monique, toward the end, and now me. At the beginning?

"Good-night, Chapman. And thank you."

He hesitated and then kissed me. First gently, then passionately. As I responded, he broke. "Good-night." And he was gone.

"Damn."

I closed the door, shutting out the confusion of my life, teetering between my need for fucking and loving—and keeping another man's love there, at arm's length.

I wanted to escape the arabesque of David and me, Chapman and me, circling inside my head. It moved like a slick, clever tongue out of my thoughts to my throat, my chest, down further. I followed ritual, my only distraction; undressing carefully, hanging up the gown, dropping my shoes on the rack, neatly folding the limp pantyhose over the back of a chair, and removing my bra last. When I was younger, the brassiere had always been first off, last on.

For the first time in weeks, I pulled on a plain cotton nightgown. Severe and unfrivolous, it was my hair shirt. I dawdled over my face, playing games with the pots of makeup remover and night cream the way a girl child might as she experimented. By two A.M. the ritual was over. Determinedly, I picked up a book and began to read, propped up in bed. I finished a page, but the words made no sense. I reread and reread, and by two-thirty I was sure I was ready for sleep.

I lay as still as possible, my eyes closed, my breathing shallow. My hands fluttered, touched, and then—like the fingers of a stranger, strong, gentle, and so knowledgeable—they pulled up the hem of the gown, spread my legs, and trapped myself between them.

It was David, having taught me how, who watched now from the foot of the bed; and in the shadows beyond, half-formed, stood Chapman.

Then as the diffusion spread up my belly, up and up, my fingers became savage. I heard, faintly, my own guttural sounds.

I came, and began again.

CHAPTER 9

THE SUN GLOW AWOKE ME. I FELT LANGUID AND SErene, like a child waking from a long illness. I lay for a few minutes without a bone or a nerve in my body; sheer, still, fluid. The alarm sounded but didn't break the mood. I sat up, buoyant, not wanting to hurry and trying to stretch out the luxury as long as possible. By the time I was dressed and ready for the day, it was almost over. The last wisp of feeling vanished as I stepped out into the muggy heat.

I'd decided to walk the few blocks to Rikki's office, but by Fifty-seventh the perspiration stained the back of my dress and prickled out of my face. I caught a cab for the remainder of the distance.

I had to wait ten minutes for Rikki, who was in conference. Nothing had changed in the cramped office. I prowled, wanting her to hurry.

"Hi, Shelley!"

"Hello, Rik..."

Too late. I had turned and answered. She was standing by the door with a grin on her face. I sat abruptly down in the chair. She closed the door a bit too carefully.

"Don't look so worried. I won't tell anyone." She went around to her chair, sat and lit a cigarette. Her ashtray was already overflowing with half-smoked stubs. "It's our secret, isn't it?"

"How did you guess?" You bitch.

"Just two and two. You're interested in Candice and Candice has an English lover who just happens to have left his wife, Shelley, and three kids." She was so pleased with her brilliance—that grin was sure to fall off her face. "I winged the rest of it. I presume you want my help?"

"Poor Candice! Was she aware that she had such a relentless enemy? And poor Shelley, too! I had no doubt that Rikki was potentially my enemy as well. It would be only a matter of minutes before I'd find out how dangerous. I had to smile. Candice and I were turning out to have more and more in common. "Yes." I do need your help, goddamnit.

"Well, I can tell you one thing anyway. Candice's business is going kaput. She's broke and depending entirely on your account which . . ." Rikki lifted her head and studied me. ". . . I gather is quite a lucrative one."

"Slightly." I sensed the direction but had no means to defend myself. "What do you think she'll do?"

"Beg, borrow or try for this job back. No way."

"There's something else." I hesitated. Could I have escaped this room without asking the question, I would have. But who else would help me? "Do you know someone called Bob? He and Candice were lovers a few years back."

"As a matter of face I do." She sat back. The smoke she blew out didn't quite veil the smile in her eyes. "But I'd like to discuss some business first."

"Of course."

"I'd like your account."

"What about Candice? Wouldn't that be . . . unethical?" I knew the futility of my questions. I asked them only to gain time to think, to maneuver myself out of Rikki's control.

"Come on, Shelley. This is New York, and we don't play cricket here."

"Pity." It didn't move her a whit. I finally nodded. "All right. On Monday I'll tell Candice." That would give me time. For what? I had no idea.

She shook her head. "I think Saturday would be better. We could have lunch, and you can give me the advance. If you do really decide to decorate the apartment, you can give me the commission letter."

"Saturday! I can't get the money so soon."

"I'm sure you could. I have to talk to Candice about some business on Saturday. So I hope we'll be able to settle it by then . . . Shelley."

I only nodded. I knew if I opened my mouth I'd scream. I couldn't think. There just wasn't going to be enough time. Oh god, I felt like bursting into tears in front of this monster. I only tried a smile and watched her scribble out something on her pad. She tore off the slip and handed it to me: the address and telephone number of one Bob Gutenber.

"Do you want to use my phone?"

"No, thank you." I rose and opened the door. She remained sitting and smiling.

"Don't forget lunch on Saturday. I'll ring at, say, eleven o'clock to confirm."

I somehow found myself on the street, walking; I wasn't sure in which direction. It didn't matter. I could just as well have walked in circles. Saturday. Saturday. Three days away. I could do nothing in that time . . . except give up and go home.

"Damn, damn, damn."

It was only when I noticed a quick sidelong glance that I realized I'd spoken aloud. I hurried. I couldn't give up. At least not yet. I caught a cab and read out Bob Gutenber's address to the driver. It was a long ride south, and I spent the time staring out of the window trying to think how on earth I could get David back in three days.

"Here you are, lady."

I got out, paid, and looked up at the towering twin skyscrapers. As I hurried across the plaza and into the soaring foyer, I tried to think up a good reason for meeting him, and of course, talking about Candice. The high-speed elevator stopped smoothly on the fiftieth floor, and I found myself outside his office with a perfectly blank mind.

The door opened and the gentleman coming out held it open and smiled for me to enter. I'd wanted to walk the corridor and think for a few minutes, but I had no alternative. The reception room was spacious. There were comfortable leather chairs, large plants and sculptures on stands. The woman behind the desk gave me an inviting smile.

"I've come to see Mr. Bob Gutenber. Tell him . . . Lady Middleton."

"Of course. You don't have an appointment, do you?"

"I'm afraid not. I was just in the area and I thought I'd drop in on Bob."

I hoped my smile was sufficiently conspiratorial. It was. She phoned through, glanced up once in puzzlement at me, then nodded.

"He's busy just now, but he'll see you in five minutes."

I took the leather chair facing the marble sculpture, which provided no inspiration. I found I didn't like it, it irritated me. I had to concentrate.

"Mr. Gutenber will see you now." She pointed down the corridor. "It's the end door." Not a long enough walk.

Thanks to Candice, I expected to dislike Bob Gutenber intensely. He was a stocky man, about David's height, and he obviously kept himself very fit. His hair was graying and receding, but his face was firm and lightly tanned. His suit fitted him perfectly.

"Lady Middleton?"

He looked quizzical and his head was bent at a courteous angle.

"Yes."

"I nearly married a lady once. I was in Oxford and it was a long time ago. Lady Julia Lambton. I always wondered—would that have made me a lord?"

"I'm afraid not."

He laughed and led me to a sofa by the window and took the chair opposite me. His view, overlooking the Hudson River, was magnificent. The Statue of Liberty was a tiny doll from this height.

"It's a wonder you can do any work."

"It's not always like this. There are days I can't see a foot out of the window. Coffee?" He rang his secretary. "I don't believe we've met before, have we?"

"No. I'm taking quite a liberty dropping in on you like this, but I met someone at a dinner party who said you'd be marvelous as an advisor for some of my investments."

"I'm afraid my firm only handles corporate portfolios, Lady Middleton. I could give you the name of an excellent firm who'd be glad to handle your financial affairs." He pulled out a small leather notebook and wrote down his suggestion. "By the way, who mentioned my name?"

"Candice Schraft."

The hand sliding the book back into his pocket hesitated before continuing its movement. He nodded. His face looked sad as he stared out of the window.

"How is she?" His voice was soft. "She's a very nice girl."

"Lovely. I know I shouldn't discuss it, but she did mention that you had once been great friends."

"Lovers, not friends." It took him some time to return to me. "I hate euphemisms. It's been a couple of years now. She's such a headstrong girl and so greedy for life. Does she . . . hate me?"

"She's not fond of you."

The coffee came and he fell silent as the girl placed the tray between us. I poured the milk, and he shook his head at the sugar.

"I'm sorry about that. I was happy when I was with her."

"Why did you break up then?"

"She consumed people. You have to give her all your time and energy. She loves doing things and kept wanting more and more of me." He shrugged. "I couldn't keep up. And she became jealous of my business and, of course, my family. They were taking up too much of my time, she said. I couldn't get her to understand that I needed space and that I couldn't just cut and run as she wanted." He looked at me and smiled. A small, soft smile. "I must sound like the bastard she no doubt described to you."

"You don't. I had thought you would be, frankly, but I only heard her side of it. She didn't mention being jealous of your family."

"Very jealous, unfortunately. She hated every minute I gave my wife. We don't exactly get on, but we are friends and I couldn't take Candice's comments on her after a while. I guess when you're young, you're insecure that way."

"It doesn't change when you grow older." I noticed his glance at his watch, but he remained attentive and polite. I liked his patience. "I think I'd better consult your friend."

"Please do. I'll give him a ring." He grinned. "That was another thing. Candice never quite understood what I did." He walked me to the door and opened it. "If you see her again, tell her . . . I said hello."

"I will."

He hesitated and then decided to walk me right through the office.

"How much did you have in mind to invest? I'd like to tell Mike to be prepared."

"Oh . . ." I waved a hand regally. "A quarter of a million. Pounds."

"Blue chip?"

"Oh yes. And some safe companies as well."

He smiled. "Mike's a fine advisor. He'll take care of it."

We passed the statue. I grimaced at the elongated sleek metal which I presumed resembled a woman. The person who'd created it had an ugly imagination.

"You don't like it, do you?"

"It . . . jars."

"I hate it myself. But my partner loves it." He stopped with his hand on the door, his head bowed for a moment. "I always thought of telephoning Candice to find out how she was. I never did, because I didn't want the whole involvement again. Do you think I should ring her now?"

"Oh . . . she's away for a week. Try her on Monday."

I leaned against the elevator wall, and thought about his remark. Jealous! How on earth could I make her jealous in the three days left. Phone David and, somehow, seduce him? It wouldn't be easy at all, and she would have to somehow know. David wasn't simple to manipulate, and he hated it to be done crudely. All my married life I'd been subtle with him, to make him feel that my want was also his. Now I had to make him not want her, and want me. God, how I needed time.

"The Plaza." The cab pulled out into the traffic and I changed my mind. I wanted the necklace repaired. It was my favorite and I loved wearing it. "No, make that Fifty-eighth and Third."

Candice's friend Anne could have been the priestess in an Inca temple: tall, rich black hair, heavy breasts, and the pallor of a jazz musician. Jewelers' eyes never leave your face, yet in seconds my worth was calculated the way a man strips a woman.

"Can I help you?"

She leaned toward me. Her perfume was sweet and heavy as a middle eastern halva. Somehow it suited her.

"I'm a friend of Candice's . . . Patricia Middleton."

"Of course. Her English friend."

She straightened, and when she smiled she was really lovely. "She told me to expect you."

I took out the necklace and handed it to her. She examined the clasp carefully.

"You really snapped this. It'll take several days . . ."

"I may be leaving on Saturday."

Anne hesitated and finally nodded. "It needs some soldering. I'll get Edward to do it now. It'll take about half an hour."

She went into a back room and I wandered around, examined by her assistant as I examined the beautiful jewels in their velvet cases. Everything looked frightfully expensive. There was one cabinet with old jewelry, including an inch-high cameo brooch. The gold was old and the carving of the woman in profile was delicate and very pretty.

"I'd love to look at that," I told Anne when she returned.

She took it out and I ran my fingertips over the carving.

"How much is it?"

"A hundred and fifty dollars."

"What's that in pounds? About ninety, isn't it?" I held it in my palm. It was so lovely. "I'll take it. And for the repairs?"

"Don't bother about that."

"Thank you, that's very kind of you. Well . . . I could come back in half an hour."

"Instead of wandering around in the heat why don't you have a coffee with me in my office?"

"I'd love that."

It was a pretty room with light beige walls, wicker chairs and wicker bookshelves. There was a formidable brown safe recessed into the wall behind her and beside it, on a table, a pair of delicate scales. I felt it all a bit over-feminine. She should have had stronger colors and furniture in keeping with the seriousness of her business. She poured the coffee from a pot steaming in a corner.

"How long have you and Candice been friends?" I asked her.

"Since school. We roomed together, then shared an apartment for a while in New York. When I got married I moved out."

"Is your husband also in this business?"

"There's no husband now. I was a musician—all I ever wanted was to be first violinist for the New York Philharmonic. When my father died I inherited this business and my husband and I had a few . . . a few? A hell of a lot of . . . differences. My divorce was a month after Candice's."

"I'm sorry."

"Don't be. My husband was a schmuck."

"Whatever he was, each time love ends, I think both the man and the woman die a little."

"I know. But it's worse when you hate each other, like we did. I still haven't had the guts to love again."

"It's easier when it ends sweetly." Praying that, whatever happened, David's and my ending would be sweet. "To love again, I mean."

Anne shook her head fiercely. "There never are sweet endings. We all tear at each other like animals."

"Candice was telling me about her David." That was hard to say. "Have you met him?"

"Yes. She's really nuts over him and Lord knows he's attractive. But it worries me."

"Why?"

"Men are such bastards and she trusts David too much. It took her a long time to recover from Bob—that's an old lover of hers—and the guys in between have been real pricks. She feels David's straight down the line, and God knows what'll happen if she finds he's been bullshitting her." She considered a moment. "But I do like him. I'm sure you would."

"I'm sure. Does she want to marry him?"

"Oh, yes. But she doesn't mind waiting."

How was I to make my beloved husband into a bastard in so short a time? To make her jealous, to make her disbelieve every endearment he had ever whispered to her?

"You're divorced as well, Candice tells me."

"No. I mean yes." Patricia, Patricia, remember your bloody story. "It's in the process."

"Candice has told me a lot about you. She likes you very much."

"Oh!" Fuck. I wished I hadn't heard that. Like Chapman's love, this would have its effects. Softening me before the kill.

"She's so excited about doing your apartment. It's an important account for her, you know. She isn't doing too well."

"But she seems so busy."

"That's Candice . . . She's got so much energy, and in this city you've got to look busy. If you don't, everyone figures you're not making it. I mean Candice is very talented but it's the wrong time. I told her that, but she's such an impetuous girl."

We were interrupted by the entrance of an old man with a strong, wise face and eyes distorted by enormous thick glasses. In his hand was my necklace. I took it. He had done a fine job—I couldn't see the break. He helped me fasten it around my neck, made a small bow and left.

"I'm sorry to hear about Candice."

"Probably I shouldn't have told you, but you're such friends . . ." She bit her lip and pulled her brows together. The deep furrows that materialized made her look much older.

"I promise I won't say a word to Candice. In fact, I want to help her. Can't she get a bank loan or something? I'm not much of a businesswoman, I'm afraid."

"She has, and that's run out. Poor Candice. Ever since college all she ever wanted was her own business. If she goes broke I'd hate to think what would happen."

"What do you envision?"

"With Candice, winning is so important. It would break her."

"You think it really would?"

"I'm sure." She watched me as I sipped my coffee. "I'm having a small dinner party on Friday, and I'd love you to come. New York is a city with a thousand acquaintances and no friends—you probably don't know too many people here."

"Apart from Candice, no. Will she be there?"

"I'm afraid not. I did ask her and David, but they said they couldn't make it."

"Were they quite sure?"

"Yes."

"What a pity. I'd love to come, anyway. Thank you."

She wrote down her address and I tucked the card into my handbag. The dinner would be a pleasant respite. Anne rose with me and walked me out.

The empty apartment was unbearable. The huge glass windows turned it into a hothouse; rather than switch on the air-conditioner, I opened all the windows. At this height, the traffic was only a gentle muttering. Tired of the view of Central Park—I saw enough of it from my hotel window—I decided to wait for Candice in the master bedroom. I followed a truck all the way down Seventh Avenue until it became a small speck, and longed for the crooked winding streets of Europe. There is no adventure looking down a straight line.

Small things are so well remembered. David's kiss on my left shoulder as I looked out of the Pension Foche onto the Place du Jardin.

David had wanted us to honeymoon in Blackpool, a seaside town with impossibly bad taste. I hadn't shuddered or protested; I had gently sulked.

"Well, where do you want to go?"

David sensed by the second week that his bride-to-be wasn't exactly enamored with the prospect of spending a week in a boarding house and eating roast beef and soggy cabbage morning, noon and night.

"The Isle of Wight."

An equally awful place, and I knew that David loathed it. Two years before we'd met, he'd visited the island with a few friends, gotten very drunk, fought, and ended up in a cell for a night.

"I'm not going back there, and that's final."

"But it's a lovely place. We can go boating, riding, we can explore and I'm sure you'd like to visit a few of your old pubs."

"Shelley, I said no."

I shrugged, obviously hurt, and looked down at my toes. My hands rested demurely in my lap. "What about Cornwall?" I sounded as enthusiastic as possible. David loved animals, wild species, but he wasn't attracted by cows or sheep or pigs or chickens.

"No." I sensed his regret. Another "no" and he would, out of guilt, begin to veer in my direction.

"I'd love to go to Blackpool then. I've never been there, and you have. You can show me the Golden Mile, teach me how to eat whelks and ..."

"We could go somewhere else. Maybe Europe. I've never been there."

Paris was easy after that. The kiss had come on the

morning after the first night. I stood at the window, sore and sticky, our greed finally having been sated at some unearthly hour. The sun should have shone, the streets should have been filled with strolling lovers. Instead, a gray autumn sky stretched out as far as I could see over the rooftops, the streets were glistening from the fine drizzle that could only be seen at a certain angle, and they were empty, not only of lovers but of people. None of which affected my mood. I was happy. I wanted to take David by the hand and, huddled under an umbrella, show him the city.

As I looked out, he awoke and came to kiss my shoulder and cradle my breasts in his palms. "I think I like Paris."

"All you've seen so far is this room. Come on, get dressed."

"Let's fuck."

"I can't just yet, darling." I kissed him and locked myself in the bathroom.

It was a three-day honeymoon; we didn't have the money for anything longer. The evening flight had brought us from London on Thursday and took us back on a Sunday. The three days, however, were not idyllic.

We had spent the occasional night together before, but then we were lovers and lovers are not people. They are the dreaming spirits within us that awake and take possession of our bodies. We lose all control as they set fires here—to our hands, our mouths, our nostrils, our hearing, our whole bodies—and there, to the mind and the heart. I do not know where they come from for at times their beauty is such that I wonder how mere people could have created them. But then, when that sad time comes, I don't know where they go to, either. Maybe like the fools we are we drive them out: preferring our dull sanity to this manic possession.

We were not depossessed in Paris but we had, imperceptibly, edged toward becoming people once again.

Mr. and Mrs. Warwick! For me it had a lovely eternal sound to it. Mr. Warwick, however, wasn't happy in Paris. I, having loved the city so long, thought everyone did.

"What don't you like?" I said over dinner on Saturday night. Even I was on edge. The drizzle hadn't stopped, my hair was limp, my shoes were soaked and, after two days of huddling under an umbrella, we were becoming a couple of hunchbacked lovers.

"The food, for one. Too much bloody garlic." He picked at the meat and nibbled at the salad.

We were dining in a self-service restaurant on Boulevard St. Germain. It was a five-minute walk from the river and, at most hours, the streets would be crowded with strollers, the lights would glisten on the Seine, and in the distance Notre Dame would soar up to a clear night sky. I could see nothing familiar in the gloom around us.

"It's tastier than boiled beef and carrots."

"Not to me." He cocked an ear at the next table. "And I can't understand a bloody word the Frogs speak."

"That's not their fault. I can translate for you. That man is saying, 'Why don't the British learn to speak our language?'"

"Yah." He grinned. "That's pretty clever. What else is he saying?"

"He says if you're going to be a millionaire by forty you'd better learn to eat frogs' legs, speak Krautese, and drink bourbon and branch water."

"And what do you say?"

"Shelley says you're acting like those silly English people who believe they still own an empire and expect everyone to speak their language."

David brooded. I thought then that his mood would last all night. I learned five minutes later that he never sulked for long, and that once he reached a decision he stuck to it.

"You're right." He was also, I learned over the years, a just man.

The doorbell must have chimed three or four times before I heard it. Candice, flushed from the heat and dressed in a beige linen trouser suit, placed a small, soft kiss on my cheek. I returned it and she held my arm a moment longer.

"I love your dress." She touched the cotton sleeves and studied the perfect cut.

"Thank you. But I must get a suit like yours. You have the perfect figure for it, of course. So many women don't."

"My extravagance for the year. It's a Lauren and I just had to buy it." She unzipped her case and pulled out her drawings.

"They're marvelous. I really mean that. Do you have any idea how much it'll cost?"

"I figure around fifteen thousand dollars. I've got it itemized here." She gave me a neatly typed sheaf of papers.

I whistled. "Couldn't you do it for less? Say, ten?"

"That's going to be difficult. I'd lose the overall effect. Okay. Make it thirteen."

"Twelve is about what I can afford."

I was feeling heady as I initialed her drawings and counted out another five-hundred-dollar advance.

"I'll give you five thousand on Monday."

By then, of course, it would probably be too late. That would be the last of my borrowed money, and I was still supposed to give Rikki something. I had no idea what. There was just enough left for the hotel bill, and I seemed no nearer to getting David back. I felt a stab of desperate pity for myself. What could I tell myself if I returned alone?

"Five thousand will be fine. Anne told me you were going to her dinner. David and I were invited too, but we can't make it. David doesn't feel like it."

Which meant, I knew, that he didn't like Anne. If Candice ever remained with him eighteen years, she'd learn that as well.

"I am sorry. I would love to have met him."

"So am I. I told David you'd be there . . ." She stared out of the window at the sharp, phallic skyline. ". . . and he was disappointed that he'd miss you."

"What have you told him about me?"

"Everything."

CHAPTER 10

HER EYES WERE WIDE AND *trés* CANDICE. "YOU DON'T mind, do you? He knows as much about you as I do."

"And what does he say?"

"Nothing, except that you sound very English."

"Anything else?"

"He said he knew a Middleton. She's a relation of his wife's."

"What a coincidence. But then it's such a common name in England."

"That's what he said as well. He was also glad there's someone left in England who's got some money. I sometimes wonder whether there's anyone left in America."

"Why, what's wrong?"

She leaned toward me and I could see the trust in her eyes.

"You're my friend, so I might as well tell you. I'm fucking broke. Your account is very important to me."

"I am sorry to hear that. What about a bank loan?"

"No way. I've already taken one. You do like my work, don't you?"

"Absolutely. What about . . ." Searching but knowing damned well what I was to say. ". . . your friend David?" One hundred thousand pounds' worth of friendship if I remembered correctly.

"The darling . . ." She turned away in time to miss the snarl in my eyes. "He made a bad investment. He came here to set up a really big business but . . ." Her thumb turned down.

"What is he doing then?" The poor dear. Men take failures into themselves the way the Japanese do their ceremonial swords.

"The same as me. Struggling. He's been trying to raise capital in London, but there's been a delay or something. Being broke doesn't help a relationship— but I don't suppose you'd know anything about that."

She studied me with soft, saddening eyes.

"I know a thing or two." I avoided them the best way I could. I prowled the bare room. There were no distractions for me, no props to hide behind. Only floors, walls, ceilings. I peered into the kitchen before returning to her side by the window.

"I can't imagine you ever being poor. You look as if you've been rich all your life. It seeps out of you and you're always so confident."

"Money helps. But you haven't exactly been poor." Remembering her professor father.

"I haven't been rich, either. My father said I'd make a million. Jesus, if only he knew how wrong he was going to be. I was going to make him so proud of me." Her eyes glowed too brightly. "And David."

He was an afterthought. It was her father she wanted to please the most.

"I'm sure you will one day. You're still a child."

"I could be dead as well one day."

"So could we all. I hope not yet." But what a pleasant thought.

In the reflection of the window, I could see her studying me. I had gotten that look often, from my children: not sly, but full of beguiling calculation. I was being weighed to help her decide whether this was the right moment to ask for something.

"Patricia." She chose her words carefully, still watching me while her fingers twisted into each other. "I know you're doing so much for me. I . . . I wondered whether you'd like to invest in my firm. You know how good I am, and I know I can make it with just a little more time."

"I'm sure you will." Her ambition was tearing at her face as I pretended to think. "I think I could manage about ten thousand dollars." The coins were my last throw. Once they were gone I'd have nothing. "What about him?"

The jugular was now within reach of my teeth. All I would have to do was snap. But I needed time. A week, not two days.

"If I give you the money, wouldn't you give him half?"

"No. Why? If he was given the loan he'd use it himself, and expect me to live off him. We have a very equal relationship."

"How nice."

I knew David would never "live off" her. He'd rather leave than be supported by her, by me, or even by his own parents.

"How soon would you be able to make that investment?"

"In a day or two. I'll have to inform my business advisors in London."

"Oh, Patricia, thank you so much. I swear you won't regret it."

"I won't."

She came quickly and smothered me in her arms. I was enveloped in her perfume, her warmth, her strength. I had to hug her in return. We broke and she moved to pick up her case. She looked like a happy, eager child wanting to run away and shout her excitement to the world. The pure light behind her gave her hair a soft, gossamer glow.

"Candice."
"Yes."
"I'm . . . I'm . . ."
"You look sad."
"It's nothing."

The hotel room was a cage. I prowled, barefoot, from one corner to the other. My teeth ached from holding my mouth open over this rich artery: one sharp bite and it would be over, and the blood would flow. And yet I was thoroughly miserable. The problem was too simple and totally insoluble.

If I gave all I had to Candice and she succeeded, it would destroy the relationship. Her success would mean David's failure. He would leave her, though not necessarily to return to me. But where else could he go? And once he'd found out who'd given the money to Candice—and that was inevitable, for "Patricia" would never survive his scrutiny—he would hate me. It wouldn't be for a day or two, or even a year; his anger at my betrayal would run deep and long. If I gave him the coins, as he'd asked me to, his success would mean my lonely journey home. I had his destiny in my hands and, oh god, I didn't want it.

At some point, when it was dark outside and dark in the room, Chapman came. I gave him a drink and sat silent, straitjacketed in worry. He talked and I barely heard him; he touched and kissed my hand but I never felt him. Finally, he shook me.

"I might as well not be here."

"I'm sorry, Chapman." Weepy and weary by this time, I told him everything.

"You really are in love with the bastard. I would have kicked him in the teeth and given her the money."

"I can't." I wailed like a Greek hag mourning the death of a child.

"Then give it to him." He said it with the irritation that only ignorance of the pain could express.

"He'll never come back to me."

"Poor Shelley." He cupped my face and kissed my nose. "I wish I were as lucky as he." He moved to the door and smiled, one of those off-into-the-sunset smiles. "I'm going to Watkins Glen, so if you change your mind . . ."

I didn't answer. It was like asking me to accompany him to the moon while I was anchored to the bottom of the sea.

"What about dinner tomorrow night? A farewell."

"Someone asked me to a dinner party. If I don't go . . ."

I heard the door close and the misery returned, settling around me like a suffocating blanket. Nothing could save me from the night. It closed in, encircling me, isolating me from the whole world. The ritual of preparing for bed disintegrated with only half my makeup removed: I swept the bottles on the dresser off in one unhappy, raging stroke. The television failed to distract me as I sat hunched in front of it, flushing vodka down my throat as if it were so much water. Fred Astaire and Ginger Rogers would glaze, fade and reappear half an hour later, still dancing cheek to cheek.

At four I rang Mother. She brought the children on before I could say two words, and they prattled on about their adventures, never hearing my sniffles. When Mother came back on the line, I told her and asked:

"Should I give it to her?"

"Don't be a fool. That would be throwing good money after bad."

"But if I give the coins to him, he won't come back."

"Well, good riddance. He shouldn't have left you in the first place. You never should have been mar . . ."

"Mother, shut up."

I slammed the phone down. She had the tenacity of a bloody elephant at times. I fell back on the bed.

When I woke up, my mouth tasting like an Algerian gutter, my eyes sticky from the night's tears, it was past noon. I creaked upright; nothing had changed. The room was there, the television was whining on, and my dilemma lay buried in my head like a tomahawk. I wandered around the room, bathed, ordered lunch and nibbled at it.

Dropping the coins on the bedspread, I stared at them as if they were tarot cards pointing the way to my future. In a way, I suppose they were. Such unattractive slugs of metal, to hold such power over my life. I picked up the phone a dozen times to ring Candice, and dropped it back a dozen times. The same number would have reached David. By the side of the phone was Anne's address. The party would be awful, but at least it would provide an escape from thinking about David and Candice.

It took me half an hour to choose an outfit. In a mood of defiance I finally decided to wear my favorite: a simple black gown and a pearl necklace David had given me for our fifteenth wedding anniversary.

By seven o'clock I looked magnificent and, as Candice would put it, self-assured. The taxi delivered me to a large, impressive building on Central Park West. The foyer seemed fashioned out of marble and brass; the elevator opened onto a small private hall. I rang, checked my face and waited.

Anne came out, took my hands, pulled me in.

"I'm so happy you could come."

I followed her toward the voices coming from another room. We passed through a lovely high-ceilinged hall lined with bookshelves on one wall and half a dozen attractive watercolors on the other. The living room was large, with huge windows looking out over the park. To one side was a little forest of plants, on the other a marble fireplace. Half a dozen men and women were turning expectantly toward me. I began to smile.

"This is . . ." Anne announced my entrance in a heraldic voice.

"Oh my god!" I stopped, one foot out.

". . . Patricia Middleton. She's from your country, David."

I was tugged toward him as he stood up and turned.

CHAPTER 11

"WHAT THE HELL ARE YOU DOING HERE?"

"Anne invited me to dinner." I smiled. "Americans are so kind, and . . ."

"Do . . . do you two know each other?" Anne's bewildered voice rose between us like a shaky white flag held aloft by a civilian suddenly caught in a crossfire. She knew the answer but didn't want to hear it.

"Oh, yes, this is my husband. We didn't expect to meet here." I extended my hand and picked up her boneless one. "I'm Shelley. I do apologize for having given you another name."

"I mean in New York?" David demanded.

My attention returned to him as Anne began to take steady steps back, her eyes searching the room. When they stopped, mine did. Candice was in mid-discussion. Too far away to have heard us, she waved happily at me.

"I came to get you." I answered it in the tones I'd answer any silly question. "You didn't expect me to just sit home while you disappeared with Candice, did you?"

I had missed his beauty.

He wasn't a handsome man or a pretty one. Only beautiful. I had carried a wispy image of this man I loved and, even at the strongest moments, I could only sense the outlines of his face and body. At other times he only existed in me, like smoke trapped in a room. I don't know why, but somehow I had expected that some indefinable change would have altered his face, that in the months since I'd seen him he would have become ugly or aged or grown some protuberance that would make him a stranger to me.

He was the same. His hair was thick and black, neatly trimmed to his collar, and in a certain light you could see the gray. The heavy eyebrows rose to sharp curves over the outside edges of his eyes. All those lashes should have curled, but men never care about such things. At times I had brushed and curled them as he lay beside me. He had protested at first—a woman's vanity—but then he'd accepted my delicate ministrations. I had never been able to make up my mind about his nose. He thought it imperial; I, fleshy. It should have been more hooked and a lot finer, to be imperial. There was a tiny scar, a crooked crescent, that could only be seen at very close range. The fading banner of a brawl, it was a source of pride.

"No, you're not that kind of woman. I wondered how you'd take it."

"Now you know."

"Yes. I should have guessed when Candice described this . . ." He gestured toward me as if I were an objet d'art. ". . . Patricia Middleton. Her style, the way she talked, the clothes . . . But that hair." He winced. "It's bloody awful."

"I like it. It makes me feel different." The familiarity of that judgment gave me an added impetus. He certainly hadn't changed, and I knew better than to back down to him. Remembering Father's advice I launched my attack with the confidence of the Light Brigade charging the cannons.

"You'll get used to it, I'm sure. Blondes really are better fun."

"What . . . ?" He began to laugh. "You really have the kind of nerve I have."

"I have much more." I looked over his shoulder and saw Candice rising. "And you're going to find that out very soon."

He glanced back. "Oh hell, I forgot about her."

The woman in question had half-crossed the room toward us when Anne intercepted and took her off to a neutral corner. It didn't take more than a few seconds. Candice's head rose slowly and she looked across to me. Her face was still; chiseled with surprise. I smiled at her, though I didn't feel in the least smiley. Biting my lower lip would have provided a more suitable expression. She looked even younger and prettier than usual as she left Anne and came toward me, her eyes wary and vulnerable.

"Candice." David took her elbow and pulled her to him. "I'd like you to meet . . ."

"I know."

I ignored the tone and kissed her cheek. Her face and neck were rigid and cold as stone. "It's so sweet of you not to be mad at me, Candice. I know I would be if I were in your shoes. I'd spit and scratch this terrible Patricia's eyes out." I hoped she wouldn't be that inelegant.

"Something like that has crossed my mind."

"No, you're too lovely to do that. Isn't she, David?" He wasn't going to sit it out in the grandstands watching us from afar.

"Ah . . . yes."

Eighteen years of knowledge was warning him what my being generous and kind meant. He wasn't to know I was teetering on the edge of a cliff.

"Would it help if I apologized? Please?"

Candice was struggling. She wanted to hate me but that could only come later. At the moment she was trying to jettison Patricia Middleton, the comission, and the promised loan for Shelley Warwick who was real, penniless, and standing in front of her.

"Thank you, Candice." I wasn't about to give her the chance to refuse. "David, would you please get me a drink?"

"The usual, or have you also changed that?"

"The usual." As he turned I followed him quickly, leaving Candice alone by the door. "You must introduce me to your friends."

"I've never met them before."

His back was to the room as he poured my drink. I faced it. There were two couples and a single man, slightly too pretty, sitting around a low glass-topped table. Anne was on the edge of a straight-backed chair, a drink frozen in her hand. No one was talking; they were all too busy staring at me. When I smiled and caught their eyes, they switched their attention to Candice and then back to me. Only the music, a Beethoven sonata, could be clearly heard.

Anne blinked herself out of her trance, smiled mechanically, went to Candice and put her arm around her.

"Thank you." I took the drink from David. We were a foot apart, face to face and totally alone. "You still are the most beautiful man I've ever known."

"If it wasn't for the bloody hair, I'd say you're the most beautiful woman." He smiled. "Guess I'm just not used to it." He moved restlessly out of our sudden intimacy. "How are the children?"

"They . . ." I hesitated, wanting him to beg for his information and making, again, the decision not to hold them as hostages. "They're very well and they miss you terribly. I left them with Mother."

"Oh, shit. I can just hear her." He tried to imitate Mother's clipped accent. "See, your father's left you. I knew it would happen and I warned your mother about marrying that man. But no, do you think she'd listen—"

"And I didn't, did I? Not in eighteen years. Even now . . ." What the hell was going to happen? I had no idea. I was playing this battle by ear, surviving from second to second the best I could.

"I'm in love with Candice." He was gentle, knowing how deeply it would wound.

"I guessed that. And out of love with me?" I waited for the decapitation.

And waited. He stood hunched, the drink in his hand, staring out of the window. In the reflection I could see Anne and Candice sitting together. Candice seemed to have recovered. She was laughing and talking, pointedly ignoring David and me.

I studied him. At times like this, I could never tell what he was thinking; his face was impassive and the eyes hooded. Eighteen years were not enough. I suddenly felt that even thirty-six would be too short, and a century no time at all. There were parts of each other we would never be able to understand.

"I don't know," he said finally. "I didn't wake up one morning and find that I no longer loved you. It could never be as simple as that with someone like you. Candice started off as a screw and she became a bit too regular. I was also getting fed up with the business. I was wanting something new and . . ."

"You got bored?"

"I suppose so." He ducked his head the way Charles did when he was embarrassed.

"How is business?"

There was one thing worse than falling out of love and that was falling into boredom. Oh god, how many times had I been bored? There were countless patches in my life where I'd lain as still as a frozen pond. I hadn't remained in the marriage out of martyrdom but because I knew when the boredom ended I would again be in love with David.

"Fine." He sounded determinedly cheerful, then he paused. "No, it isn't. That's why I need the coins."

"Are you in a lot of trouble?"

"Let's say I was overoptimistic... I sank my capital into a factory, but the others haven't come through as yet." He was going to add something but it turned into a Gallic shrug. "I guess I'd better join Candice."

"You'd better." I touched his sleeve. The Doug Hayward suit that I'd given him for his thirty-ninth birthday fitted him really well. "You can pick up the coins from the hotel in the morning." I wanted to get away from him as quickly as possible, but he held me by my wrist.

"Thanks, luv." He looked over my shoulder in the direction of Candice.

"She told me you were going to invest in her business. You could have, you know, and I couldn't have done anything."

"I also know what would have happened." I touched him on the cheek. It felt faintly rough and so warm. "I'd prefer you whole with her than in pieces with me."

I could have made my exit on that grand line, sailing out of the apartment and out of his life forever. But that would have been a retreat, and the empty chair at the dining table a symbol of my rout.

David left my side and I tried to look self-contained. It was too lonely. I was aware of myself moving toward the pretty young man, and somehow I managed a smile.

"I'm Shelley Warwick."

"And don't we all know that by now, my dear. You've given Anne enough cardiac arrests to last her a lifetime. I'm Hal." He took my glass and refilled it. "You are staying for dinner, aren't you?"

"I was invited." I hoped the fatigue that was slowly creeping through my body wasn't showing.

"You certainly were, but as someone else."

"I walked in as someone else, and she went right out

the window. I hadn't expected my husband to be here."

"Candice changed his mind at the last minute, and I bet Anne's wishing she hadn't."

"And Candice?"

David sat by her in a distant corner, huddled in a conversation I wished I could hear. David touched her hand. David bowed his head and their hair touched. David talked. David . . .

"She's fucking mad. And she's called you a few names I won't repeat." He raised his glass and I found myself liking him more. "You're quite a lady."

"Thank you." I returned the salute and felt slightly more buoyant. "It wasn't fair, was it?"

"For whom? Candice? Don't expect me to weep for her. She knows there's nothing fair in life."

I thought walking into the room and finding David was the unfairest of all.

"You must really love the guy."

"Yes, I do. And that's the easiest confession I've made in my life." The intimacy of that confession nearly made me burst into tears. "Let's talk about something else. We're at a jolly dinner party, aren't we?"

"It's going to be tough. You're the main topic of conversation."

"We'll try. What do you do?"

"Paint, but unfortunately not for a living. I lecture to earn my crusts of bread . . ."

In victory, we all become possessive. Candice slowly lifted her head, looked straight at me, and took David's hand. If it had been possible she would have held him aloft like a trophy.

"You're not listening, are you?"

"I'm sorry. My mind was wandering."

Anne came in to announce dinner. Forgetting my misery, I was absolutely famished. No one dies from love or sadness or bereavement or loneliness, however much we may wish to at the time.

"I guess mine would too." Hal walked with me toward the dining room.

David detached himself from Candice. He never liked being clung to under any circumstances, especially in the presence of strangers. Another habit she had yet to learn.

Anne tugged Hal away from my side the moment we entered; I felt like a soldier suddenly stripped of protective armor. The dining table—mahogany, well loved and polished—shone warmly in the soft lights. A middle-aged black woman, gray-haired and weary, stood by a door at the other end of the room. She wore a neat blue dress that looked like a uniform. I smiled at her. We were both so alone in this room. At first she didn't respond; then the smile came to her face faintly, as if it had traveled a great distance.

David came to my side and surveyed the room.

"She thinks I knew it was you all the time."

"Why on earth should she think that?"

"Well, she'd described Patricia Middleton to me, the way she talked, her style, her mannerisms, her clothes, and she thinks I should have instantly recognized you from her description. Silly bird!"

"I hope you didn't call her that." He had shown me her Achilles heel. I would only have one strike at it.

"No." He laughed, I smiled. "It took me a bit of time to persuade her that I hadn't known it was you. I said there were twenty-five million women in England, quite a few of whom are upper class. So someone called Patricia Middleton walks into New York and commissions you to do something. How the hell do I know it's my wife? I hadn't met or talked to her. She finally accepted it all."

"I should hope so." Knowing full well that we never truly believe others once we have reached our own conclusions.

"It took some fast chat. American women are so bloody insecure."

"We all are, and bastards like you are the reason for it." There were moments when I wanted to kick David in the balls. This was not one of them. "And God help me, I love you." It was said as softly as possible so only he could hear me.

He stood still, not turning to look at me. Watching his profile, I knew my declaration had been made too suddenly for him to protect himself against those words. They hung like silk threads between us, holding us together. I waited. It was up to him to brush them away so he could escape forever.

"I know." He didn't move; it seemed he was savoring the words.

"Does she fuck as well as I do?"

"Not yet."

"She never will."

Anne came between us, awarding David a smile and me an appropriately dirty look.

"David, you sit there . . ." She pushed him away from me and in the direction of Candice, who had adopted the policy of ignoring my presence altogether. "And Shelley . . . you here."

The three of us were seated on the same side of the table, a husband placed between me and David. Hal sat on my left, at the head of the table.

He rolled his eyes comically. "Anne had ulcers trying to figure out the new seating. You were originally placed facing Candice, who wasn't to have been next to David."

Hal was the ideal dinner companion, determined to entertain me and relieve Anne of some pressure. Over a delicious minestrone he told me sly stories about art and theater, moving on to high-level gossip with the roast and baby onions and the final course which was served rapidly—coffee with, not after, the perfect lemon soufflé; our hostess standing before I'd managed a sip.

Hal pulled back my chair. "Could this be a hint for us all to depart into the night?"

"I think so. And Hal, thank you for looking after this fallen woman."

"Look, this is the most interesting dinner party I've been to in years. Wives don't walk in on straying husbands *every* day." We were back in the sitting room, and I could hear the "good-byes," loud and clear, behind me.

"I hope we can meet again. Why don't you give me your number?"

"Sure." He wrote it down on the back of Anne's card and gave it to me.

One of the couples offered me their quick, limp hands; I shook them though we hadn't exchanged a word. Anne had my purse in her hand, and I took it as David came up to me. Candice was sitting in a chair, flicking through a magazine.

"Will you be able to get back all right?" he asked.

"Why? Are you proposing to take me back to the hotel?"

For a moment, I thought he was. He seemed to waver, then glanced at Candice. I didn't envy him the rest of the evening.

"What time shall we meet tomorrow?"

"We shan't. I'm away for the weekend. I'll leave the coins for you in the hotel safe at the Plaza." I turned away from him. Anne was holding the door open. "On Monday I'm returning to London."

"Where are you going tomorrow?"

"Good-night, David." He kept half a pace behind as I moved to the door.

"Anne, I'm so sorry to have spoiled the dinner."

"I hope I never have to go through that again."

"I would like to have a quick word with Candice. To make my apology, of course."

"She won't talk to you."

"In that case I just wouldn't dream of leaving." I pushed the door open wider and waited.

CHAPTER 12

I COULD HAVE WAITED FIVE MINUTES OR FIVE HOURS. David remained faithfully by my side, talking. I barely heard him. I needed all my concentration for what was to come.

Candice came to me finally, reluctance in every step, her face tight as a mask.

I smiled at her. "You understand, don't you?"

I stepped into the tiny hallway and pressed the elevator button. It had to come on time. She remained on the threshold, poised and ready, her anger barely controlled. She was determined to concede no ground.

"I don't."

"Oh, I'm sure you'd do the same thing if you were in my shoes. After all you did get yourself pregnant once, didn't you?" The elevator door opening behind me made the only sound. She was not going to say a thing. I stepped back and smiled over her shoulder at David. He returned it. Perfect.

"It was such a lovely surprise seeing you again, darling."

"Again?" She snapped and turned and caught his smile.

"Oh!" Mother would have been proud of that one: So full of surprised faux pas. "I meant since London ... of course."

The door closed and the elevator began to drop. I heard the apartment door slam on the scream: "The bitch."

The charade was finally over, and I was exhausted. The doorman found me a cab and I fell back in the seat, feeling as if blood were trickling out of my veins. A slow steady stream that would soon leave me unconscious.

Back at the Plaza, I checked Chapman's room. He was out. I left a note: "Collect me on your way to Watkins Glen. Shelley."

I had made up my mind when I'd told David I would be away for the weekend. I needed a respite, a diversion, before returning to the children. I would spend tomorrow shopping for gifts and then enjoy two days of being loved and needed by a man.

My room closed in on me protectively. I unzipped the black dress, let it fall and kicked it toward the cupboard. The shoes flew in the same direction. I felt as wrinkled and limp as a used stocking.

Shelley ... Shelley ... you shouldn't have.

What? Gone to dinner? Come to New York? I threw the shouldn't to the wind and yanked my suitcase out of the closet.

Chapman phoned while I was hurling balls of clothes into it. The smaller case, for the weekend, would be packed neatly.

"I got your note ..."

"Don't tell me the invitation list is closed, Chapman."

"Oh Christ no. I just wanted to say we're going to have a marvelous time. And to thank you."

"Don't you want to know why I'm coming?"

"No. I learned a long time ago to never ask a woman like you 'why.' Good-night, Shelley."

I slept the moment my head touched the pillow. It was all over, like death, and I had no worries left. Defeat and victory are so final that either one must bring sleep.

I awoke suddenly, full of anticipation and impatience. It was a sunny, cloudless day and I jumped out of bed. It was only seven-thirty; I tried not to hurry as I bathed, exercised and dressed. By nine, I could stand the suspense no longer. I rang Hal.

"It's Shelley."

"Don't you women ever let a man get his beauty sleep? Candice called me at eight, commanding my presence. The dear child knows I never wake before ten, and after that exciting dinner last night I needed a Librium. I feel awful."

"Never mind your problems, Hal. What happened?"

I heard him sigh and yawn. "Since I'm up, I may as well come round to your place. The Plaza, isn't it? That's on the way to Candice's."

I ordered a fresh pot of coffee and waited. It took him an hour and a half, and I had the door open before his finger had left the buzzer.

"Easy." He moved carefully and sat delicately on the sofa. "I'm most fragile this morning. It's a wonder I can even stand."

He didn't look fragile, though the dark glasses hid his eyes. The smile on his face was conspiratorial and I poured the coffee as calmly as I could, but the cup and saucer rattled as I passed it to him.

"Well?"

He was sipping too calmly and ignoring me. "Stop hovering. My nerves are absolutely shattered. Just sit down . . ." He patted the space behind him. ". . . and I'll tell you all. And I mean *all*."

I sat and waited, my arms crossed. Oh god, it had to have worked. There was no second chance. Everything depended on how Candice had reacted to the thrust.

"The scream and the door-slamming didn't help one

bit." Hal had to begin at the beginning, and I knew he intended to savor every moment of the telling. "Candice was literally shaking with rage. She should have looked magnificent, but she didn't. There was a sort of ugliness to her mouth and for a moment I thought she was going to have a fit. You, I imagine, would have been all ice and crackingly beautiful. She just boiled." He patted my knee affectionately.

"What was David doing?"

"I'm coming to that, if you'll wait. Candice called you a fucking bitch, then a cunt. She must have a limited obscenity vocabulary—that was the extent of it. Then she went over to the bar and poured herself enough brandy to knock over a marine, my dear. David wasn't sure whether to defend you—I think he was quite lost in his admiration of you—or to side with Candice. He tried the typical British compromise; he said nothing. But he did go across to her."

"You could replace Hedda Hopper, you know." I stood up. The sitting was making me too restless.

"I'm her reincarnation. And if you're going to pace, please do it behind me. I hate being distracted. Where was I?"

"David..."

"Oh yes. He tried to hold her, she screamed. 'Don't you dare touch me.' She was getting some control over herself, but I do wonder what some of us would do without the old movies writing our dialogue. Candice took another slug of the grape. 'You knew all along that bitch Patricia Middleton was your wife, didn't you?' She looked better now. Quite beautiful, really. David had this paternal look on his face, and I guessed he was going to humor her. Fatal, my dear, fatal."

I stared out of the window. "He never does that with me. We fight."

"He knows how to handle you, but Candice in ways is still a stranger to him. I could have told him she loves confrontations. David makes it worse. 'Don't be silly. I didn't know it was her.' No good. 'Of course you did. How long have you been seeing her, and for God's sake tell me the truth this time, you bastard!' David was very calm, which infuriated her. 'This evening was the first time I'd set eyes on her in New York. You told me you'd met this woman called Patricia Middleton and that she was going to be your bloody savior. I had no idea it was Shelley.' Candice wasn't having any. 'Fucking liar. She told me she'd seen you. I heard her.' David was beginning to lose his patience, and he made a mistake. 'She's a clever woman and . . .' Candice pounced on that line. 'And I'm a dummy, I suppose.' "

I smiled. "That was a mistake."

"Shelley, stop interrupting. Who's telling the story? You or me?"

"I'm sorry, Hal. Go on."

"Candice was positively snapping now. 'Shelley's not clever,' she said. 'She's a fucking viper, and she was helped by someone. She knew who I was, what I looked like, what I did. Someone fingered me.' David just shrugged. If he'd agreed with Candice about you, the whole thing would have blown over. But he wouldn't. He just smiled gently while she was raving about you, and that only goaded her on. 'I'm going to get that fucking wife of yours.' My dear, Betty Bacall couldn't have delivered the line better.

"I think David was beginning to worry for you. He told Candice to let you be, that you were going back to London on Monday. Candice was pretty far gone by now. 'She's not going back thinking she's made a sucker out of me. Nobody does that to me.' Well after that Candice just became silent, in a dangerous steaming sort of way. David was worried—he kept whispering to her, and all she did was shake her head and keep saying 'I'll get her.' "

"You don't believe she's going to shoot me, do you?" I hadn't thought of that possibility. It made me feel . . . not afraid, just uneasy and sad for Candice. I stifled *that* feeling quickly.

"I've no idea what she's going to do. But she's such a silly girl. She has David and can keep him if she stays cool, but she wants revenge." Hal carefully placed the cup and saucer on the tray and stood up. "Last night she just left him standing in front of the empty chair, kissed us good-night, and stalked out. She was out and in the elevator before David had straightened. I don't think he's the kind of man who lets his women walk out on him. He spent about five minutes more with us, chatting, and then went out." Hal kissed my cheek and we both moved toward the door. "Now I have to go and find out what Candice has plotted. I think it's going to be a marvelous day for me. I love conspiracies."

"You'll let me know what's happening, won't you?"

"Of course. But don't expect me to take sides. I'm a fence-straddler until I know who's won. then I root like hell."

"How sweet of you." I pushed him out. "Ring me."

The moment the door closed, I did a little skip. It couldn't have worked out better—so far. The more extreme her behavior, the more she would force David to defend me.

I waited, trying to read while watching the telephone. An hour and a half later, it rang. I grabbed it and answered; it went dead. A half hour passed before it rang again. This time it was Hal, who seemed to be phoning from the center of a traffic jam.

"Where are you?"

"Outside the Plaza." He had to shout them twice before I could distinguish the words.

"Well, come on up and tell me what she's doing."

"I can't. She'll see me. She's standing half a block away, watching the entrance. She doesn't know I'm behind her. She isn't armed—unless you count the St. Laurent suit, an Hermès scarf and a cloud of Calan-

171

dre." He giggled and I winced. "It's so exciting. She has hatched up something but she won't tell me what. That's why I'm following her. I think she's waiting for you to come out. She wanted me to arrange a lunch with you. No way, I said."

"You didn't tell her you saw me, did you?"

"I'm as clever as I'm pretty. I've no intention of getting caught in the crossfire."

I listened to the traffic over the phone. If she was waiting for me, I could keep her waiting forever. But I needed her to carry out her plan. That was the only way to draw her out into the open.

"What happened at her place, Hal?"

"Thought you'd never ask. She was very calm and beautifully dressed. I asked her where David was. The sofa was, well, not exactly unmade, but it looked distinctly used. 'Work,' she said and then the floodgates opened. Jesus, did she get mad at David last night, and as for you, she's still calling you names and wanting to tear your hair out. When she stormed out of Anne's last night she couldn't find a cab, so by the time David went out she'd calmed down. But what got her going again was that he was worried about what she was going to do to you. That made her furious—and she didn't even know what she wanted to do, except kill you. You see, she'd built up this relationship with you, and it turns out you're her worst enemy..."

"How's she getting on with David now?"

I tightened my grip on the phone and pressed the receiver hard against my ear.

"I asked her that. She said she'd been so sure of him and now she wasn't. She knows it's all happening in her head and in one way she feels he didn't know anything. But the problem, my dear, is that you knew who she was, what she did, everything. Of course, the shit hit the fan when she phoned her father and they matched descriptions. She figured then that David had told you all about her. She swore at him, threw him a blanket and locked herself in the bedroom with a bottle of cognac."

I laughed. It would have been delightful to see.

"How did David take that?"

"Philosophically, I gather. But he didn't get too much sleep."

Hal stopped too abruptly, and I sensed he was not wanting to hurt me.

"Go on. I can take it."

"Well, by about two Candice had worked something out, but now she needed David to forgive her. So she woke him, sweet-talked him and they made love. She said it was part of getting back at you."

"I wish you hadn't told me."

"You did ask."

"I know." They'd been making love for weeks, of course, but that had been distant, part of their past. This hurt.

"I'm sorry, Shelley. Anyway, she asked me to make a lunch appointment with you. Not asked, pleaded and cajoled. Thankfully I'm immunized against women. Did you get a call and have someone hang up?"

"Yes."

"That was Candice checking to see if you were in. Then she phoned David and very sweetly suggested they have lunch. She wouldn't tell where, said she'd decide later. She made it sound urgent and very important. I gather he said yes. When she went out I followed her and here I am."

"You've no idea what she's going to do?"

"None. I told her I'm excellent for advice if not for action but she told me to stuff it. That sounded exciting. It's your move next, Shelley."

"Thank you, Hal."

I sat for fifteen minutes by the phone, desperately unsure. How much had they kissed and made up? Why was it always my move? I wished some deity would reach down and take control of all my affairs—I could blame someone else then for any mistakes I was to make. I had to be sure that what I did was going to be absolutely right.

I went to the window and peered down. No familiar woman, no Hal. I cursed. I had forgotten to ask him what colors she was wearing.

Well, if I had to show myself . . .

I grabbed my purse and decided to shop as I had planned. The crowded streets would offer some kind of protection, and the shopping would give me time to prepare. I stopped on the steps and adjusted my glasses. I could still see no sign of her or of Hal. Strolling toward Fifth Avenue, I stopped often to stare into the windows. I thought I glimpsed her once when I quickly turned, but I couldn't be sure. I shopped mechanically—a small camera for Charles, toys for the girls, a lighter for Father, a necklace for Mother—with my head constantly revolving. Could she and Hal have made up the whole story? He was, after all, her friend and my acquaintance.

At one-thirty, I turned down Fifty-fourth Street. It was emptier than Fifth Avenue, and I hoped I could spot her. She might as well have been a professional detective—I couldn't see her anywhere.

"To hell with it." I turned into the Dorset Hotel and headed straight for the bar.

I sipped my Cinzano and soda and sat back, enjoying my favorite hot-weather drink. I was grateful too for the air conditioning; inelegant at the moment, I flapped my arms and unstuck my dress from all the places it was sticking.

I was seated with my back to the window, next to the glass partition that gave a striped view of the bar and the entrance. The packages were arranged around me like crackling children, and I toed both shoes off and flexed my feet. The relief! The quiet room calmed and soothed me. It resembled the bar in the Connaught, and the old waiter hovering a few feet away reminded me of Father's old batman. Solicitous but not servile.

Halfway through my drink, I glanced toward the bar and the door. Candice and David, refracted by the striped glass, were just entering. She clung to his arm and, despite the glass, I knew she was looking straight at me. David at her.

"Oh, shit!"

The waiter, used to czarinas, closed his eyes and moved a foot further away. I positioned a menu at forehead level seconds before they passed. The maitre d' moved ahead of them, and, on Candice's orders, seated them almost diagonally from me but six tables away. Candice made David sit with his back to me. She held his hand, she touched his face and his arms.

Momentarily, I lost them. They became blurred, wavery shadows in the lights which now hurt my eyes. I bowed for my handbag and groped for a Kleenex.

"Is Madame all right?"

Blinking, I saw only the black shoes and trousers in my clearing vision. The voice was soft and concerned.

"Thank you. Could I have the bill?" He hesitated a moment, as if he wanted to touch me, and then he was gone.

I would have gone too when he slid the paper in front of me. Except I had nowhere to go, and leaving would mean conceding victory to Candice, and remaining a mute witness to her affection was entirely too painful.

I had no alternative. I stood up, forcing Candice suddenly to react to my presence. She waved and blew a kiss.

"Could you take my drink across to that table?" She was such a child in warfare. I could be magnificent. "And the packages, please."

"Yes, Madame."

I allowed him to precede me. He pulled a chair up to the table for two and waited.

David was just turning around when I leaned down and kissed him on the mouth.

"What a lovely surprise to see you both." I pecked her cheek and sat down as the waiter pushed my chair in. "Thank you."

"Madame is welcome."

"Shelley!" David's surprise was genuine, not part of her trap. "Where the hell did you spring from?"

"I didn't spring, David, I was sitting over there."

The waiter brought the packages, and I turned my attention to Candice. David needed space and time to arrive at his own conclusion. I began to smile when her eyes dropped to her left hand, resting too far forward on the table. She was toying with a large engagement ring on her third finger. It glittered like a tear drop and seemed to catch all the light in the world. When I managed finally to lift my eyes, *she* was smiling.

Oh god, Hal hadn't told me about that. What else had he withheld? I glanced at David. He wouldn't do that. Would he? What else had happened last night?

I managed a sip of my Cinzano, then pulled the camera I had bought for Charles and thrust it in front of David before she could mount her attack.

He took it and held it almost tentatively, as if he expected it to explode. He was looking not at the camera but at me. Out of the corner of my eye I saw Candice reach for his hand.

"How long have you been here?"

"Sergei, when did I get here?" I turned to the waiter as David raised an eyebrow. "He reminds me of Alton, with a touch of Chekhov." I smiled at Candice. "Alton was my father's batman. There was no Robin."

"Half an hour ago, Madame."

He was better than Alton—he'd exaggerated by a few minutes. David glanced at his watch and looked up at Candice. Her smile didn't waver.

"Oh, *Sergei*." She made an effort to mimic me and nearly succeeded. "Please bring Madame another drink. We want to celebrate something, don't we, darling?"

David continued frowning a moment, then finally nodded. He was turning to me, about to speak, when Candice leaned over.

"To our future, my dearest." And she kissed him, her mouth lingering on his.

CHAPTER 13

DAVID PULLED BACK AS IF HE'D BEEN BITTEN.

I turned away. I felt as if I were in bits—heart, soul, thoughts, words, life itself were falling, tumbling, breaking. I had to make a final effort. I pushed myself upwards. "I'd better go." I signaled the waiter, who scooped up my packages.

"No, don't." David half rose, wiping at his mouth. His hand gripped by Candice, who was looking at me and laughing.

"I was going to tell you," he said. "My first contract came through, and I won't..."

"How nice!" I bent over Candice suddenly and pecked her startled cheek for the last time. "I hope your father wasn't too angry with me when you spoke to him last night," I said softly.

Candice jerked her head away. "Who told you I'd talked to him?"

I put on my dark glasses and smiled. She turned and looked at David, who was preoccupied with trying to attract my attention.

"Shelley, listen..."

I touched his face, acknowledged the maitre d's

quick bow, and I was out in the heat without once looking back. As I was signaling for a taxi, Hal touched my arm.

"You must tell me all about what happened inside."

"Ask Candice." I was halfway into the cab when my momentum began to run down. I stopped. "I'm sorry, Hal." I kissed him. "You've been so sweet."

"Do you want me to come with you?"

"Thank you, but no. I'll be all right. I'd better be— I've got a big weekend ahead. I promise I'll tell you later what happened."

When Chapman knocked on my door at three o'clock I wasn't ready. My face needed patching. Fifteen minutes later, looking the best I could, I met him in the foyer. As I approached, I felt like a girl about to surrender her virginity. It wasn't that I had forgotten our previous weekend, but this encounter was somehow different. As was this Shelley also about to be a different person.

"I'm sorry." I kissed him quickly on the cheek. "I figured you'd be late." His happiness at having me with him made him look younger, lighter. "So we're still on schedule. The plane's waiting for us at LaGuardia."

"Oh god, it's not another helicopter?"

"I won't do that to you again. It's a Comanche, and you'll be quite safe."

"Okay. Do you know where we'll be staying? I'd like the hotel to know where to contact me in case Mother telephones about the children."

He scribbled out the name and number and waited while I left careful instructions as to how I might be reached. And the coins, neatly wrapped—for David Warwick, much love, Shelley—with the manager.

In the taxi, Chapman took my hand and kissed it. I let him keep hold, feeling once more the need to abandon myself to this man. I was sure of our fates only for the next two days, but if we wanted it, those days might become our forever. I did not try to convince myself that this was what I really wanted: it was all the possibility I held at the moment. I sighed, and Chapman turned my face toward him and kissed my mouth.

"What's up, Princess?"

I remembered now that he'd called me that in Monaco as well. He probably called all his women "Princess," but I was feeling too drained to care.

"Do you sometimes feel that you've done everything short of moving mountains, and nothing happens at all?"

"Often." The cab hit a deep pothole and we bumped against each other. "This is one of those times for me as well." He glanced at my hands. "You're not really here with me, are you?"

"You've got my hand." I smiled, but he didn't return it. "That's all the flesh and blood I have. There's nothing more of me hidden away in the hotel room."

"You know I don't mean that."

"I can't forget him overnight, can I?"

If I ever can. For a moment I wished I could spirit myself into their lives and see what was happening. No, I didn't want that. One can only take so much destruction.

"Did you make any progress?"

"We met at a dinner party by accident. We talked."

"And?"

I looked out without answering. I was surrounded by the inhumanity of high-rises and eight-lane highways, frightening and intimidating me. Surrounded by such unyielding brutality, how does one love?

"Did you give him the money?"

"Yes." I avoided his eyes, sensing pity and, then, the sly spark of elation. Another bloody victor.

"So we have a happy ending. He's got the girl and the money and . . ." He stopped too suddenly.

"And you've got me. Is that what you were going to say?"

"Something like that." He made me feel like a primitive conch shell that had just been bartered. "He's got no reason to come back to you now, has he?"

"None."

"There's going to be plenty of time for us." He lifted my hands to his lips and held them there. "This is going to be the best weekend in my life."

He gave me a brilliant seducing smile and I laughed. My god, they were all the bloody same. But I did need him.

The helicopter ride that night at least took place in the dark. In broad daylight, this plane looked as if it had been assembled by Charles from one of his kits.

"Are you sure it's safe?"

"Of course it is, Princess. Come on."

He climbed onto the wing and pulled me after him. I stepped as lightly as I could and sat carefully next to him in the cockpit. He strapped me in, then crackled away to the control tower. The moment the plane began to move, I shut my eyes.

"Are we okay?" I opened one eye.

"Safe as houses."

I opened the other. The sun was unnaturally bright and clear; the soft white clouds above my head seemed near enough to touch. Chapman smiled at the nervousness he saw on my face. It took me ten minutes of staring at the sky to work up the courage to look down.

"Can't you climb to the same level as a jumbo? I can see people's faces."

"I could make it up a bit more, but thirty thousand feet? We'd freeze to death." He rested a hand on my knee and began to caress the insides of my leg.

I removed his hand, kissed it and placed it back on the stick. "I'm not saying I don't like it, but I'd prefer both hands at the controls."

"I could loop the loop if you want."

"Don't you dare."

By the end of half an hour I was beginning to enjoy

myself. The noise of the engine was lulling, and I felt like an overlord of the world. It was so lovely and lonely. I wished I could be by myself, floating skyward forever.

"Could Betty pilot one of these things?"

"She was one of the best. I taught her. Want to try?"

"Not yet."

He became entangled in his memory, and I didn't distract him. In the faint reflection of the window, I could see his soft smile: these were happy times he was remembering.

"Once when I'd had a shunt at Brand's Hatch and broken my right arm, she flew me back to London. It was a bloody awful day. We had high winds and rain and the visibility was poor. I thought she wouldn't be able to do it." He shook his head in admiration. The poor man still loved her. "She got me down safer than I could have."

"It would take a thousand years to teach me how to fly."

"It's simple."

For the next fifteen minutes he tried to show me how to fly the damned machine. I had been cast in the role of Betty—not that I could blame him. Like generals who spend their lives fighting their previous battles, so do lovers fall in love with their past love. We want to duplicate our boyfriends, our lovers, our husbands, to find in one a quality recognizable in the other.

In Chapman I could catch the glimpse of familiar humor, the same strength and determination, the same boyish eagerness as David's. I wondered what of Betty was reflected in me? It couldn't have been my ability to fly this plane. It would be something else which only he could see.

"Are you getting the hang of it?"

"No." I kissed him. "You may as well give up. I have no intention of learning."

182

"What would happen if I broke my leg?"

"We'd take the train, Chapman. I'm a lousy pilot but I excel at buying tickets."

We bickered, lightly, both trying to keep our pasts from suffocating us. Surprisingly soon it was time to land; as he swung over a river, I shut my eyes until the plane came to a complete halt.

Watkins Glen was a small pretty town that flashed by my taxi window. The hotel was spacious and cool. Part of some endless chain, the one he always stayed in whenever he visited. He'd booked us into a double room.

"I'd prefer singles."

"Oh, come on, Shelley."

"I don't mean to be difficult, I just want two singles. I'll be at your beck and call whenever you want, Chapman."

He would have argued, but he knew it would be futile. We signed the registers separately and I kissed him back into a good mood in the elevator.

The room was plastic wood paneling, color television and a miniature bathroom. The Gauguin reproductions on one wall lent a small air of dignity to the room. Chapman knocked and entered.

"It's depressing." I pulled the blinds closed. The room looked much better gloomy. Sunlight was too real for it.

"If you'd been in as many of these as I have, you'd be used to them." He chose a corner and began undressing, quickly and neatly. "The only way I can tell the difference between cities is to look at the telephone directory."

At times, men make me envious. They don't have breasts that will sag, nor do they worry over stretch marks on their stomachs. Our bodies are like clocks; in the mirrors we can watch them running down. Chapman was slim-thighed and flat-bellied. His hips may have pouched slightly, but not enough to make him look any less athletic. Even his damned wrinkles looked youthful. His cock felt the same to my touch.

"God, you're beautiful, Shelley."

That was all I needed. If he remembered me differently I never heard him in his whispers, nor in the gentle way he touched and kissed and felt. There was the experience of countless women in his fingertips, and in the weightless movement of his body above mine, and in the way he held and cradled me as I came. He kissed me gently back to the surface. He was also, thankfully, a man who never asked whether a woman has come. He would instinctively know. As would David.

"I hope we're going to spend the rest of the days making love," I said.

"I wish we could, but I have to work." He got out of bed and began dressing. "Would you like to come to the circuit with me? You've never been in the pits, have you?"

"I have in the theater."

He threw a pillow at me. "I'll show you a whole new way of life."

"You've made a good beginning. But don't expect me to get dressed as fast as you."

"I've got to meet James and some of the others. I'll see you down in the bar in half an hour."

"Make it forty-five minutes."

A quick kiss and he was gone. I lay in the tiny bathtub, wanting only forgetfulness. The lovemaking had certainly relaxed me, yet my mind was struggling to escape the confines of Chapman. I dressed quickly in a trouser suit and a yellow silk blouse, the only casual outfit I had with me.

Chapman was sitting at a table with five other men. When I reached them, he jumped up and introduced me. I suppose I might have recognized the Jameses and the other names, but I didn't. Charles should have been with me: some of them were his heroes.

I had entered a world composed of special men. It only helped to intensify my loneliness. In a language I did not understand they talked of other men I didn't know. They also loved each other deeply. Years of bars and strange cities and deaths bound them together: even another male would have found it impossible to surmount this barrier. A woman was a universe away.

Chapman tried to pay attention to me. He would break off his conversation to explain and to include me in their talk, but once we reached the pits I was forgotten. Betty must have loved him enormously to have withstood this isolation for so many years.

I had forgotten how ugly and phallic racing cars were. The pointed oval-shaped nose flowed back to the vast lump of an engine. The driver of Chapman's car looked eighteen years old. They all looked like boys playing with new and frightening toys. I had also forgotten the noise. Each time a car passed a pit, my eardrums threatened to burst.

Peering down the length of pits, I could see other women. They all looked elegant and, like me, very alone. At the end of fifteen minutes my head began to ache. I was only sitting and waiting for Chapman, the way I sat and waited for David.

"I'm going back to the hotel." I screamed into Chapman's ear. He only nodded. If he'd asked me to stay, I might have.

The sun was still warm by the time I reached the hotel. There was a miniature pool behind it; I changed into a one-piece and swam a couple of lengths, then settled back to read a paperback.

I felt mentally suspended in the nitrous cold air of waiting. War wives, sailors' wives, racing drivers' wives, salesmen's wives, housewives, mistresses: we are all bloody Penelopes waiting for our Ulysses. And we do it because we want to, which is the worst part.

Chapman joined me by the pool as the warmth of

the sun began to fade. He looked flushed and happy. For a while he had returned to the only thing he deeply loved.

"I'm sorry you didn't like it out there." He draped his coat over my shoulders, kissing the right one first.

"To me, it's noisy and boring. All the cars do is go varoom. I don't know how the other women stand it."

"They want to be a part of what we do."

"They never will be, will they? It's just a game you let them play."

"It's not a game." In the shadows I could see his mouth tighten. I offered a smile but he chose to ignore it. "Betty would keep lap times and she knew a bloody lot about the cars."

"Lap times! You mean pressing a stopwatch every time you zoom past? My ten-year-old daughter could do that." I sat up straighter and winced as my bottom touched a cold, wet patch. "You'd never get me trailing around pits pressing a bloody button to prove to myself I was a part of you."

"That's because you don't want to take an interest in what I'm doing."

"Oh!" I was certainly getting to be as good as Mother. "And when I go out painting no doubt you'd come and hold the palette. And whenever Betty did whatever she liked doing, you'd drop everything and join her?"

"If I felt like it."

"This bloody myth of togetherness makes me yearn for the days of division of labors and pleasures. Thank God David never asked me to go and sit in his office or watch him play football."

"Maybe that's why he left you."

"He doesn't have that fragile an ego. And if he's suddenly developed one with Candice, he'd better stay left."

Chapman didn't answer. The poolside lights came on and the water looked clear and pretty. The blur of light and shade added an awkward grace to the ugliness that had surrounded the pool. The softening of the landscape also softened my mood. I touched Chapman's hand and for a moment it lay still.

"I don't know why we're arguing, you know."

His hand stirred and finally responded. "I was hoping you'd love motor racing the way I did." He pulled me to my feet. "You never will, will you?"

"I could get to dislike it less, given the time."

We walked back to our rooms and I hoped I'd never have the time. Being with one man when I wanted another was making me feel miserable and I shuddered at the thought of feeling that way all my life. Thinking I was cold, Chapman put an arm around me.

"You won't have to put up with it as much as Betty did. It's only occasionally that I visit the circuits."

"I'm glad."

He stopped at my room and began to enter with me.

"What time are we joining the others? I assume that's the program."

"Just a few of us, really." He had the grace to look apologetic. "I thought we'd have a drink at eight and then dinner."

"In which case we have no time for a quickie. Knock on the door and I'll be ready." We kissed and parted.

I knew I'd drink too much that evening. It was a party of eight. Four men, champions of one time or another, and their wives—mistresses, or whatever. I was sure only of my own identity: mistress tempora or possibly something more permanent. I felt indifferent to my fate. I was the stranger. I had seen two of the women in the pits and they obviously knew each other well. They gossiped and swapped jargon with the men. The third female—titian-haired and post-adolescent— was Frank's one-nighter. I was, I suppose, also in the same category if you looked at it from her point of view. I reached for Nirvana: tall and cold, with plenty

187

of ice. By the time we were ready to leave for dinner, three had slid down my throat.

"That was pretty fast." Chapman was looking disconcerted as we trailed the others out to the car park.

"You're not the only one who can go varoom."

There were times, so rare, that I had done this with David. Usually, when I was very angry with him.

"I just hope you know when to stop. I don't like women drunks."

"And I don't like men who don't like women drunks." He stopped and seemed to be wondering whether to take me back to the hotel.

"Don't you ever have times when you want to get high?"

"Yes."

"This is mine." I pulled his face down and kissed him passionately. "Take care of me, Chapman. And don't remind me of anything in the morning."

When I pulled away, he nodded and touched my hair. He could be a darling man.

The other cars started and drove off. Chapman opened the door for me, and then just sat behind the wheel. His face, in the shadows, was changing. He seemed somehow to age as I watched; the wrinkles around his mouth grew fractionally deeper.

"Shit!"

He started the car and pulled out onto the road. The passing cars threw snatches of light across his face and each time it seemed even more immobile. He didn't even wince at the suddenness of the glares.

"Just try not to call me David."

"If I do, forgive me." I held his hand to my cheek and he was gentle enough not to pull it away.

"Will your mother really want to know where you'll be?" He turned and looked at me. I shook my head. "And she won't worry about double rooms either, will she?"

"Are you angry with me?"

It took him a minute.

"No."

The club where we were to dine looked popular. There was hardly any parking space, and we drove a couple of circles before Chapman found one. I took his hand and held it tightly as we walked into a pretty room with a large fireplace at one end and a large black man playing romantic tunes on a piano at the other.

"Do we have to sit with the others?"

"I'm afraid so." He smiled but there was little humor in his eyes. "It may be the last time."

Chapman, as far as I can remember, was the perfect lover that evening. When the time came he carried me back to my bed. This last I presumed, since I awakened in it.

The blinds were drawn but the sun penetrated the room with thin lances of white light. I lay back gently. My memory felt like the broken bits of a jigsaw puzzle in which most of the pieces were lost forever. We had made love, at least I felt quite sure we had, and I wished I'd been more conscious to have given Chapman more enjoyment. He had said he loved me. It must have been often, for the words stood out of the blur. I couldn't remember what I had said or what I had called him.

It took me another couple of hours to sit up and swing out of bed. I felt a little better, almost human again. There was a note on the table.

"Gone racing. Back sixish. You were marvelous. P.S. You didn't get me mixed up with someone else."

"Thank God." He had enough of his own pain.

By the time I'd bathed and made up, it was four-thirty and the sun no longer had the same devastating effect on my eyes. I picked up the paperback, put on my darkest glasses and went down to the pool.

Scattered around the pool were women, a few children, and a young Adonis showing off dives. He was the type whose virility lies only in his biceps. I chose a lounge chair as far away from him as possible and settled back to read. It was warm and peaceful, and I must have slept deeply, for when I woke up the sun was nearly down.

There was a man's shadow lying across my stomach and for a full minute, as I watched, it didn't move. The Adonis, no doubt.

"Go away."

"I really fancy you, luv."

David sat down on the chair beside me.

CHAPTER 14

"WHAT?"

"For a wife."

"Haven't you used that line on another . . . chick?"

He laughed. "Not quite. I've been looking for you. I'm glad I found you."

"So am I."

I kissed him, went straight to Chapman's room and knocked. He opened it and stepped aside. It seemed as though he'd been waiting for me.

"How was the racing?"

"Fine." He turned away, took off his jacket and put on another.

"I'm sorry, Chapman." I reached out for his hand but he wouldn't give it to me.

He moved further away and toward the door.

"Maybe we can meet for another weekend in another town."

"You wouldn't like that."

He hesitated and then came to me. An arm went around my neck and he touched my mouth.

"I wouldn't. I saw you by the pool with a fella. Was that him?"

"Yes."

"He doesn't look like that much."

I laughed. "Chapman, not every man can be as handsome as you."

He smiled, touched me again and was gone. The room felt suddenly desolate, and I hurried out. I didn't start packing immediately.

David would wait for me in the car; stepping into it would be like returning to the familiar comfort of driving home together again after a late party.

Now, I needed a few moments to think, to regain my breath. Oh god, the price we pay for loving, and it is never-ending. What would there remain of me at my death but the faintest strain of the innocence I had been born with? There was never enough time to prepare, but this would have to do.

I sat for fifteen minutes, a respite before the next eighteen years.